OLIGARCHY

Also by Scarlett Thomas

Fiction
Our Tragic Universe
The End of Mr Y
PopCo
Going Out
Bright Young Things
The Seed Collectors

Non-fiction
Monkeys with Typewriters

OLIGARCHY

SCARLETT THOMAS

CANONGATE

First published in Great Britain in 2019
by Canongate Books Ltd, 14 High Street,
Edinburgh EH1 1TE

canongate.co.uk

1

British Library Cataloguing-in-Publication Data
A catalogue record for this book is available on
request from the British Library

ISBN 978 1 78689 779 4
Export ISBN 978 1 78689 802 9

Typeset in Baskerville MT by Palimpsest Book Production Ltd,
Falkirk, Stirlingshire

Printed and bound in Great Britain by Clays Ltd, Elcograf S.p.A.

For all my family, and particularly in memory
of my aunt Ines Troeller

She starts two weeks into term, on the wrong day, when everyone else in her class has been at the school for four years. Her plane lands on a rainy evening and while other people close their eyes during the turbulence she presses her face to the small window and sees London. London! Its smeared varicose veins below pulse with moneyed fluorescence. She is not afraid of turbulence because her father would never let anything happen to her, because he understands the fluorescence, and he is almighty.

In the car that takes her to Kings Cross, the driver, a shrivelled man with a baseball cap and a deep voice, starts talking. They are in some kind of underpass which looks as if it might go on forever and then doesn't. None of the vehicles are moving. It's all so clogged. Atherosclerotic. A heart attack waiting to happen. A—

'Yeah, I got a Zombie Slayer,' he says, slow and sonorous. 'It's a large knife, like a machete with a serrated edge. I got it with me now, if you want to see it.'

Some fight-or-flight hormone – whatever you call it in

English, the thing that makes you fat if you don't act on it – begins to burn in her but then goes out like a match fizzing in the rain. He can't really have just said that? But perhaps dying on a slick dark night in London would be interesting. Efficient. And she would not have to lose her virginity, or learn how to use eyelash curlers, or ever go home. Still, she tilts forward a little in her seat. Manages to swirl up a few more hormones. At the next red light, she could—

'But I need you to know that I don't want to kill anyone. That's not why I carry a knife. But of course a lot of people who don't mean to kill actually do, because once you've got a knife you can't help it and . . .'

Yes; she could probably jump out. These doors are locked, right? But only so people outside can't get in. She could leave any time she wanted, like in that film. But what about her massive suitcase? This road has no obvious pavement. How would she climb over the barrier? Is this how people actually die, worrying about silly details?

'You need to understand that of all the young people caught up in this lifestyle, ninety per cent are coming from fatherless households.'

What? OK. Right. It's not her cab driver talking; it's the radio. A call-in programme about knife crime in the city, one of the reasons her mother did not want her to come here. The useless chemicals in her body swirl like flower petals and then sink into the mysterious darkness

2

of her insides, along with the Diet Coke she had on the plane, and the half lemon, and the one vegan salted caramel chocolate that she hates herself for right now, even though she threw the rest of the box away.

On the train north she worries about being raped by the unshaven man sitting opposite her. Why is he even in the first-class carriage at all? She has a large Americano that she bought from the English coffee kiosk on the platform at Kings Cross. When he goes to the buffet she puts one of her long, dark-honey hairs on it, so she'll know if he's tampered with it when she goes to the toilet. But when she comes back the whole cup is gone, and there's an East Coast Train employee limping up the carriage with a large fluorescent bag that is not full of money.

*

Her name is Natalya but at home they call her Natasha, she explains. Like in *War and Peace*. Or Tash, which is more English, apparently. Her thighs are massive. The French girl in her dorm, Tiffanie, is demonstrating how, if you stand up straight with your legs together, you should be able to see three diamonds: ankle to calf; calf to knee; and then between your thighs. She says much of this in French, which no one seems to mind. Your thighs should not touch each other anywhere, not even if you were born like that. Everyone tries it, apart from

Bianca, who is absurdly spindly and has more diamonds than you are supposed to have anyway. Tash has the right proportions, although her thighs are still massive. They are nowhere near as big as Rachel's, though. Rachel is huge and doughy, with an enormous Roman nose and a fuscous moustache that she has to wax. And then there is Lissa, who is sort of greasy all over, like she has been smeared with butter.

Natasha does not yet know her way around the school, a vast country house with attics and turrets and ghosts. It is on the edge of a village that has a church, a shop and a phone box that now functions as a miniature library with books that smell of drunk boys' piss. The school's main staircase is haunted by the White Lady, whose portrait hangs there, and student WiFi is only on for an hour a day, between six and seven. How are you supposed to do anything with only an hour a day of WiFi? The girls compose emails offline and then hit *send* in a wild stampede at six o'clock that sometimes crashes the WiFi and ruins everything for everyone.

They – the boarders, the imprisoned – are perhaps the only people left in the country who are so antiquated that they still use email, but there is no other choice. After the stampede they spend the rest of their hour downloading music, and streaming like crazy. You can't get Instagram or Snapchat offline, but there are two or three celebrities whose feeds and stories are compulsory, to whose lives an hour a day of access is not enough.

4

The girls are not allowed on YouTube because they are too precious. They are not allowed to upload anything, ever, because their lives are still little foil-wrapped secrets. They hear of new platforms and apps, but what are you supposed to do when you are locked up in this place with its wood panels, heavy curtains, dangerous tasselled rugs, BO and acne? Who needs group chat when you are a group that chats anyway, like IRL, like literally all the time, even in bed?

Danielle lives in the village. She spends every evening in the Year 11 common room half in the IRL group-chat and half creating capsule wardrobes on Pinterest for holidays she will never go on, to Abu Dhabi and Kenya. She goes home just before it gets dark. Tonight, in the bad corner of the common room by the ancient CD player and the old beanbags with the period stains, Lissa manages to get a search result on antique erotica, despite the 'parental' controls. For some reason the only images that make it through are of big-arsed women with enormous dark bushes, which Donya says will turn them all lesbian, which means wearing horrible boots with laces and driving your own car. There are no penises. Tits everywhere, of course. Strange stomachs that must be over 35 per cent fat. Skeletons, for some reason, looming. Fainting couches. Bianca is like a looming skeleton herself. She leans over like a damp paper straw and types something into Lissa's iPad and lo there are some cocks, although one looks like a carrot and the other is on a boy who looks about twelve. They are line drawings, not photographs. Woodcuts, FFS.

Tiffanie gets out a Sherbet Fountain, which she calls a 'dib-dob'. She eats all the sherbet and saves the liquorice stick to hide in Donya's bed. Later, while trying to remove some of the grease from her forehead with a cotton wool ball, Lissa whispers to Tash that Bianca has secretly joined a Pro Ana WhatsApp group and spends all her time in the loos puking, which is why she has such bad breath. She adds that Bianca also does not TePe daily. Outside the windows is a dark silence, the dark silence of English villages in autumn, the barest sound of leaves fluttering to the ground and the last wasps sucking out the insides of the last plums, and mysteries in the depths beyond the gloom.

These two dorms are stuck together out of the way, in one of the old turrets. They have sloping ceilings and shiny wooden wardrobes with little brass keys. Tiffanie, Lissa and Natasha are in one; Donya, Rachel and Bianca are in the other. It's as if they were put here for some deliberate reason, to make them feel different from everyone else: to make them go bad. Then again, things stored carefully in dark remote places are not supposed to go bad, are they? Like apples; and potatoes, which are apples of the ground, according to Tiffanie.

Before lights-out, Rachel has a bath, and then offers Natasha the used bath water. Is that what they do here? Should she accept to be polite? But she has never done that. She is not polite, not any more. And just imagine what there would be in someone else's bath water. Pubes. Microbes. Bits of fuscous moustache. So gross.

'No thanks,' she says.

Rachel smiles. Natasha has passed the test. Tiffanie has Marlboro Lights hidden in the top of Donya's wardrobe, foreign ones without pictures of desperate old people's black lungs and missing toes. Does Tash want to go to the woods with them tomorrow? She does. It's damp and mossy and English, English, so fucking English. But the smoke reminds her of her father, and home. It tastes how he smells. She remembers his aftershave, and the haze of his big cars with the leather interiors, and the way he loves her more than he ever loved her mother, or his last wife. He loves her more because she is his own flesh and cannot ever betray him. Because she is new. And because she is thinner.

*

Horse-riding is on Sunday morning, after church, a blur of girls in green felt capes and the death-ray stares of villagers who hate them. In the dorm Natasha's thighs look like prize-winning hams in her pale jodhpurs. She has to stand on her single bed to look in the wood-framed mirror on the wall and she notices then how her fat wobbles. She has never seen her fat wobble before. She is thinner than her mother but her fat still

7

wobbles. Is it because she is standing on a bed? But everything looks wrong here in the strange low light filtered through ancient dust and history that is different from home.

The stables are also different from the ones at home. The horsesmell is the same, but here everything is done by red-faced village girls who work in return for free rides at the end of the day. They talk all the time about the rich girls who own the horses but never ride them. They look at the girls from the school with bafflement and pity. First of all, because they are rich but don't even own horses. They have to come here and ride tired old Min and moody Lucky and restless Pablo, who has that mad look in his eyes. They can only ride once a week! No one trusts them with anything, and they aren't even allowed to tack up.

Natasha is given Pablo, possibly as some kind of prank, but she controls him easily. She knows how to talk to animals so only they can hear. To Pablo she says things like: *I know how you must feel, because you were expensive once and now you've gone a bit crazy and no one cares about you except for a lot of stable girls with bad clothes and fat mothers.* And he understands that they are the same, that maybe she too has been sent to this place to die, and so he canters for her in a way he won't for anyone else and everyone is impressed but Tash just shrugs. She still doesn't know why she was sent here, to this remote, dowdy place. There is cheap, watery hot chocolate afterwards, and village boys, of course; village boys are everywhere. It's just that no one ever sees them.

*

On Monday everyone starts a new diet. It's Lissa's invention.

The diet is this: wholewheat bread and Sandwich Spread only. No butter. Vegetables are allowed but no fruit. And no potatoes. Natasha has never had Sandwich Spread. It's English and gross, like cold sick. At lunchtime they ask for vegetables only and old Mrs Cuckoo the cook rolls her eyes and laughs at them and saves them extra treacle tart for dinner, which by then they all eat, except Bianca, who crumbles hers into tiny pieces that she feeds to the birds.

Late at night the girls do their secret things, after telling each other stories of the village boys. The village boys howl outside the windows after lights-out, like wolves, because they are so desperate for it. But from whom, exactly? Not Rachel, whose dark regiment of pubic hair has paraded shamelessly up to her belly button and down her thighs. Not Lissa, whose T-zone cannot be absorbed by all the cotton wool balls in the world. Not Donya, whose underarms smell of offal. Tiffanie: yes. The village boys would probably kill for Tiffanie, with her B-cup French breasts and shiny hair. Maybe that's why, when everyone is asleep, they bay at the windows like beasts; perhaps it's all for Tiffanie, or perhaps now some of the

9

clamour is for Natasha, with her odd purity, her dark-honey hair and blank blue eyes. Her ability to ride.

Bianca doesn't care about the village boys, and so when everyone else is asleep she sneaks out of the old servants' door and does star-jumps in the moonlight while bits of dandelion clock and fairy circles whirl in her head.

*

The White Lady is called Princess Augusta. There are pictures of her everywhere. The biggest one is on the wall opposite the grand staircase, facing you as you come down. It depicts her in a flowing white dress, with a turban, holding a large harp between her legs, its shiny head nuzzling her right breast. The dress makes her look immense. For some reason she is wearing sandals with it, and sitting by an enormous pale classical column which reflects the light in a way that does not flatter her. The light instead picks out the complex black jewel in the turban. The jewel sucks in the light and absorbs it and hints that it is gone forever.

Tash finds Bianca at the bottom of the stairs gazing at a smaller portrait of Princess Augusta, aged fifteen, looking almost pre-Raphaelite with her halo of pale physalis hair and her pomegranate lips. The odd jewel is there, this time on a choker. Her skin is smooth and powdered like white marshmallow. She is not wearing a bra. Natasha suddenly realises that Bianca has exactly the same halo hair and is about to say something when Bianca glides away, sits at the grand piano and starts playing Chopin.

The dark eyes in the painting are like polished lychee stones. They are saying 'Make me.' They are daring, dangerous eyes, especially for a fifteen-year-old. They are saying, 'Go on, then. Do it.' The jewel glints in the same way.

The story the girls tell on the rare nights when there are no village boys goes like this: the man who first owned this house was called Sir Brent Spencer. He had high cheekbones and a pure white beard and kept a nightingale in a turquoise cage. He was in love with Princess Augusta, but as he was a mere commoner they were not allowed to marry. Instead, they lived in sin and he died clutching a simple silver locket containing her picture and then she drowned in the lake beyond the sheep field. She had been ruined years before by the sultan who gave her the black diamond, but Sir Brent Spencer didn't care.

Did her hair look like that while she was drowning? Did her eyes? Did the locket tarnish until it was turquoise like the bird cage and then crumble into dust?

Tash wants to ask Bianca for directions, but Bianca has her eyes shut, her narrow, ravaged body bent like a claw over the piano. Her arms are like brittle talons. She is the only girl who does not roll up her regulation green kilt to mid-thigh. She instead wears hers absurdly long, ending mid-calf.

11

Where is the Porter's Cabin? It's apparently where the post comes. If you have post you get a notification on your School Tablet. There is no map on the tablet, and the school is a complicated burrow of stairs and passageways and back-stairs and servants' areas, some reserved for Year 10 and some reserved for Years 12–13. Tash can't find the Year 11 stairs and then takes the wrong door down the wrong flight of stairs and ends up in a cold boot room surrounded by lacrosse sticks and carrier bags and a couple of sulky Year 10s giving her The Look. The Look says, *Who the fuck are you?* It says, *Why are you here?* It says, *You're lost, and we're not going to help you.* It says, *You're new money. You're foreign. You're a Jew. Your father is an oligarch and you don't even know what that means.*

Back up the stairs and through a different doorway and into the wide corridor that leads to the front door that nobody uses. The headmaster's study is here. Outside his door it smells of coffee and old wood. Is she allowed to be here? She isn't sure. Tash hurries down the corridor before anyone sees her, past more pictures of Princess Augusta, and a framed list of School Rules. One picture of Princess Augusta shows her in the lake, floating on her back holding a withered rose in her pale dead hands. Outside the windows are the gardens with their bright green grass and geometrical hedges, all draped with new cobwebs.

By the time Natasha gets to the Porter's Cabin, the one-hour allotted time for picking up post has passed, but he gives it to her anyway. Why is this? Is it the way she bites her lip and looks like she might cry? But she doesn't let that feeling into her eyes. Her eyes express something else entirely.

*

It's a letter, from Nico. The envelope is thin, and smells of his mother's cheap Russian cigarettes, the only ones you could get during communism. He's got the address of the school slightly wrong. His handwriting looks like that of a slow child who has only just learned English letters. On the back he has written his address across the seal in Russian. Natasha hates him so much. She hates him for being innocent, and Russian, and poor. She hates him for his cheaply cut thick hair, and for his pathetic aspiration to be a martial arts sensation on YouTube and eventually move to Moscow. Not Paris, not London. *Moscow*. She hates his saliva, the memory of it. His white socks.

She hates the pact they made, that they would only communicate by letter from now on, because why? Because people might read the emails? Because the servers might go down? Because anything might collapse at any time: the electricity companies owned by the oligarchs, or capitalism. Capitalism might be the next thing to go. But the postal service? Natasha hates Nico's faith in the postal service.

13

She hates his belief in aliens.

His cold face.

His bitten fingernails.

His small hands.

*

Another trip to the Porter's Cabin. A parcel from Tash's father. At last. She hasn't heard from him in weeks, not since the visit when it was decided about the English school. It's a pair of boots in a wrapped box. No one in the school is allowed to order anything online: all parcels must be sent from home. But you can't buy these boots online anyway: they have long since sold out and there is a lengthy waiting list. They are from the Balenciaga shop in Moscow, where someone knows someone who . . . In Moscow, 'knowing' sometimes involves guns and threats but not in Natasha's world. Not yet. Not that she knows of. But anyway, why has he bought them in pink when she specifically asked for them in white? She sighs and asks who wants them, these useless millennial-pink sock boots in a size 39.

She thinks her father would like this: she's sure of it, in fact.

Danielle's eyes are wide. The boots cost a thousand pounds.

Natasha gives them to Tiffanie, and at six o'clock she emails her father for the right colour. She complains to

14

him about the email system here. About the food. It's all so fattening, she says. So English. But she will probably get into an English university; that's the main thing. And she'll try out for the sports teams but she won't develop too much muscle.

The next day a padded envelope arrives. The porter raises his eyebrows. So much post for the sexy Russian girl. Inside the envelope is a book of Chekhov's short stories in the original Russian, and hidden in a hole cut out of the story 'Peasants' is a thin, shiny, silver 5G-ready iPhone which connects to a secret network and allows its owner fast unlimited internet access for free, wherever they are in the world. It has an Apple Music account activated, which is useful, and an app called DarkWeb, which is frightening. The phone has been set up so its owner can look at literally anything: beheadings, anal penetration, how to make bombs. Not that Natasha would want to look at those things, of course. She really only wants to look at girls who are about the same shape and size as her wearing clothes she hasn't thought of wearing. And boys with longish dark hair and freckles. And fierce-looking ponies.

Sellotaped to the back of the phone is a black Amex card in her name, and a note in Russian, in handwriting she doesn't recognise, saying, 'Buy anything you need with this. You may not hear from your father for a couple of weeks, but don't worry.' The card is more solid than other credit cards: harder and more lustrous.

Natasha hides the phone and the black Amex in the secret compartment in the lid of her trunk that her father showed her before she came. 'If you have to hide something really dangerous,' he once told her, 'put it in someone else's things. Some secret place they don't even know they have. And then say it's theirs.' She has thought about that a lot. When he first said it to her she didn't know what he meant, but she does now. It's a bit like Tiffanie always hiding cigarettes in Donya's wardrobe.

That night Lissa goes looking for porn again through the school's WiFi. Today, she manages to force through the parental controls some Victorian charcoal illustrations of a fat man in a top hat waving his massive dick at a frightened servant, and a woodcut of a Japanese man penetrating a peasant who has her legs tied to a broom handle. His penis is enormous.

'Is that what they really look like?' asks Danielle.

'Haven't you ever seen one?' says Lissa.

'Have you?' says Danielle.

'Of course,' says Lissa. 'Hasn't everybody?'

No one actually has, except Tash. And even then, she didn't really see it.

After lights-out everyone has something glowing under their sheets. They write to parents, siblings, attractive cousins; they listen to podcasts to help them sleep. They listen to music they have downloaded earlier. Then there are the secret things. And the things that are too banal to be made public. Tiffanie listens to French pop music and plans her modelling career, and then her wedding, and then her funeral, which will have a botanical theme.

Bianca has downloaded *Fanny Hill* for free and has found details in it far more troubling and thrilling than anyone could discover with a search engine. But she does not tell anyone about it, because she does not really tell anyone about anything. She doesn't tell anyone about the sadness and the failure and the light inside her that is a bright white colour but is never bright or white enough. She doesn't tell them that she wants a black diamond like Princess Augusta's that will take the light away, and purify it, and make it better.

*

It is Exeat, which is Latin for getting the fuck out of here, and means a weekend at home. Some of the girls can't go home, because home is too far, and so they stay. Tash gets a day out in London with a glamorous aunt she's never met. The aunt, Sonja, is in cyber-security, or something like that. She has her own company. It turns out that she is the one who sent the iPhone. She is Natasha's father's sister.

'Well,' says Aunt Sonja, kissing Tash on both cheeks, when she meets her at Kings Cross. 'You look adorable. So fresh and young. Like a flower. I've been absolutely dying to meet you. Why did your mother hide you away for all these years, huh?'

17

Aunt Sonja has a car with a driver parked outside the German Gymnasium. They are driven to a Chinese restaurant down a back street behind Tottenham Court Road that smells of incense and is full of millionaires in white jumpsuits drinking jasmine tea and eating lotus-bulb salads.

Natasha feels empty and vaguely rotten inside. To her it is older people who look best. They have wisdom, experience. They have had proper sex. They know how to use make-up. They can go out in the day and buy useful things. They do not have to go to school, and no one tells them what to do. They can flaunt their power. Get fat. Spend whole days alone and naked. They can buy horses and diamonds without having to ask anyone's permission. They can get piercings and dye their hair. They can talk to people without blushing, without the words cracking halfway through. They know who their parents are at all times. Even wrinkles are attractive to Tash because they talk of real life and age and know-ledge. All she wants – what she yearns and yearns for – is knowledge. She doesn't know *anything*. Well, nothing useful. She particularly does not know how to talk to this woman, with her blow dry and smooth forehead and perfect pink nails.

Aunt Sonja looks more like a young person than old people usually do, and this means that she spends thou-sands of pounds, Euros and roubles each month on every tiny part of her. But nevertheless something about her still looks wise. Is it in her eyes? Is that how you tell someone has knowledge and experience?

'I don't know how to talk to young people,' says Aunt Sonja. 'It's been so long. I don't even talk to clients' children now, although I used to enjoy scaring them.' She winks, and Tash notices that she has somehow managed to put mascara on in such a way that each long, black silken lash is separate. When Tash puts on mascara it just clumps into a massive dead squashed spider.

Tash tries to smile encouragingly; she raises her shoulders and it comes out as a shrug. Aunt Sonja has been speaking Russian but now switches to English.

'You are not on social media?'

'No,' says Tash. 'I mean, only to follow people, not to post. At school we're not really allowed. At home I . . .' She shrugs again. How to explain home to this person?

'Good.' Aunt Sonja switches back to Russian. 'In my job I come across – used to come across, because now I do more blockchain work – billionaires' children who had no clue. They'd put up pictures of the family castle on Instagram. The helicopter they were flown there in. Names of pets. Pictures of the interior of their bedrooms. The names of their gyms. Their personal trainers. They may as well have sent out invitations to be kidnapped.'

Natasha shudders. But she's in the UK now. No one kidnaps anyone here. That's what her father told her mother. He is almighty, and it is OK. Also, Tash is here

19

because he is super-cautious, not because he's in any sort of danger. And she has been invisible all her life so why not just stay invisible now? And prepare for the future: university at Oxford or Cambridge, followed by—

'Can I curse in front of you or are you too young?' says Aunt Sonja in English.

'We swear at school,' says Tash in Russian. Then in English: 'It's OK.'

'Fuck and cunt, or just fuck? I need to know where the boundaries are.'

'Whatever you like.' Tash blushes like a pathetic child. She wants her aunt to say cunt; then again, she doesn't. Or fuck. At least she's not saying them in Russian, which would be awful. Something about swear-words in other languages is amusing and comfortable. Tiffanie says *putain* all the time, which is French for 'prostitute' and is apparently one of their worst swear-words. *Putain, merde*, she says, every time she drops something in the dorm. *Putain mer-DE*, she says, emphasising the last syllable of the word so it sounds like *murder*. All the other girls say it now too, whenever they want to swear.

Aunt Sonja looks at one of her pink nails as if seeing it for the first time. 'What do you talk about with your friends? Boys, I suppose. Diets. Shoes. Ha!' She laughs. 'Just like we did.'

But surely it's not like it was? Despite her talk of social media, Aunt Sonja has that quaint air of someone who

20

grew up before memes and YouTube families. How can Tash explain that in conversations nowadays boys have been reduced to their body parts, or really just one body part, and that her friends' diets are so secret and weird that you could never, ever discuss them with an adult? Why is that? Because they are ridiculous. Because their diets, and everything they think, and everything they do, is ridiculous when compared to real life.

For Tash, real life is somewhere between a known unknown and an unknown unknown. Categories which are themselves unknown unknowns. Well, sort of. Her father said something like that once, didn't he? The first meeting or the second one. Last year.

'Do you look at porn on the internet?' asks Aunt Sonja.

She blushes. 'No. We try. But no.'

'It's corrupting. Don't. Use your iPhone to shop for clothes and cheat in exams.'

'OK.'

'Have you had a lesbian experience?'

More blushing. 'No.'

'Do it. It's underrated. But not with someone from school you have to see every day. I'll call someone. Someone discreet.'

'Nono. You really don't have to. Please. I'm—'

'Look at your beautiful skin . . . I didn't appreciate my skin when I was your age.'

A pause to finish digesting the lesbian comment. For it to be processed and removed.

'Your skin is nice too.' It is. It glows in a way that is unnatural but all the more beautiful for that.

'But yours. *Fuck.* It's the skin of a baby.'

But everyone has it, this skin that says *I'm young and I know nothing.* Literally everyone she knows apart from Lissa has the same skin – even Lissa's would be OK if she used the right toner – and so to compete she needs something else. Why do adults not understand that? And it's not boots from Balenciaga, either. It's nothing you are born with; nothing you can buy. You have to go into the woods and fight monsters for what she needs, but no one will let her, and she doesn't even know where the woods are, if they are even in this country, and these new monsters might actually be real and—

'I want to give you some advice,' Aunt Sonja says. 'Ask me anything you like.'

How do you . . . ? Tash shrugs yet again. How do you be interesting without having to be a lesbian? How do you style your hair? What are you supposed to think about at night? Why did my father ignore me for the first thirteen years of my life? But the words don't come.

'All right, then. I'll tell you what I wish someone had told me when I was your age. Do everything you can to keep your beauty. Exams are not important. If you're clever it'll show anyway. I wish I'd done less studying and simply learned more about people – this is a skill you need in the real world, trust me. Take off your make-up every night. Moisturise. Exercise. Never let your

22

skin see the sun. You can take vitamin D intravenously instead; I'll give you the number of the clinic I use in London. People think it's vanity to worry about beauty when you are beautiful naturally and you don't have to. But I guarantee you that when you are my age you would rather spend the day in an art gallery, or recline in a garden eating persimmons in the dusk, or lie around reading stories set in the tropics in a silk dressing gown without having to spend all your free time in fasting clinics like your father's ex-wife does. And your mother? I assume she still does that too? I haven't seen her for so many years. Anyway, if you put the weight on once you will never, ever take it off. Well, you can do it temporarily, but once it has been there it will always long to return, like a missing lover, like a weed, like a boy gone to the army. So you have to avoid it.'

'How?'

'Don't eat before lunchtime. Ever. Well, only fruit. Not bananas or dates. Never drink alcohol – it's empty calories. If you need to relax, try chamomile, meditation or Valium. If you really want to try drugs don't buy them from some tragic dealer in a nightclub – call me and I'll find you something safe and untraceable. The rest is common sense. Don't have too many calories but don't have so few that your body decides to hoard all its fat. Have two meals a day. No sweets. Brown things, but not chocolate. That's it. Save your brain for important matters.'

23

'OK.'

'And always carry this in your handbag.' Aunt Sonja gives her a small red can. It says *Deep Heat* on it. 'If anyone ever tries to attack you, spray this in his face.'

'Deep Heat?' she says, reading the label. It's in English.

'It's stronger than normal Deep Heat,' says Aunt Sonja. 'It's Russian. Be careful with it. Spray him first to stun him, then call me and I'll have him killed.'

'OK.'

Aunt Sonja smiles. 'You think I'm serious?'

'I don't honestly know.'

'Well, hopefully you won't have to find out.' Aunt Sonja sips her jasmine tea. 'And how is your mother?'

*

Somebody in a long-ago government decided that girls should read classic feminist literature and so they are studying Angela Carter and the school can't do anything about it because it's the law. The English teacher is called Mrs St John, which is pronounced Sin-Jin. She is extremely old and has a pink rinse and sometimes falls asleep in class, clutching at the pearls around her neck as she dreams, no doubt, of kidnap and servitude. She smells of rabbit fur and gin. One story has the word cunt in it. Another has cunnilingus performed by an animal. In fact, the licking of animals features in several of the stories. Girls have their skin licked off, or have

24

their hands licked while they are resting in their laps – their *laps*, which means . . .

'Do any of you girls know where the word cunnilingus comes from?' asks Sin-Jin.

Nothing moves in the room except for fifteen pairs of beautiful eyes that look down, or from side to side, or simply widen. Is a teacher really talking to them about this? Now?

The girls are doing Bianca's diet this week. Everyone thought Bianca's diet would be basically nothing, but in fact all they are eating is cake. Bianca is throwing hers up, of course, but she hasn't mentioned this to the others. And in any case, dieting is all relative and one of the most effective ones (the Einstein Diet, haha) involves simply making the people around you much, much fatter. Bianca feels particularly real this week. She is luminous; whole; sparkle-filled. It's as if she can see things others can't: the invisible connections that bind us to each other, to our decisions, thoughts, friendships, strategies. She's a weightless comet blazing through the dark sky; a fictional character; a wisp; a dream. She persists now only on puffs of icing sugar: the stuff that gets inside your blood before you can do anything about it.

She flies . . . And then *falls*. She flies . . . And then *falls*.

Each time the fall is greater, and each time the flying is higher, and the sky gets darker and darker until it seems entirely black and endless and—

25

'Well?' says Sin-Jin.

'Princess Augusta doesn't like it when we talk about cunnilingus,' says Lissa.

'She thinks it's vulgar,' says Danielle.

'Except when Sir Brent Spencer does it to her,' says Rachel. 'Or the sultan.'

The other girls giggle. Someone makes a slurping sound. Tiffanie says something like *le sexe oral* in her growly voice. Sin-Jin is trying to ignore all this in that way adults sometimes do, but it just gets the girls going even more. Goading someone who is not reacting is often even more fun than goading one who does.

'Sir Brent Spencer was secretly gay,' says Bianca. 'He also liked bestiality. He once sucked off a horse. That's why Princess Augusta drowned herself. Because she liked it too. She *loved* sex after she was ravaged by the sultan who gave her the black diamond and—'

'Right, that's it.' Sin-Jin has finally snapped. 'Headmaster's office. Now.'

*

It's Monday, and Natasha's turn to invent an eating plan for everyone to follow. It is the most elaborate so far. Even Bianca looks interested in it. Tash repeats the list of what they are not allowed to eat. *Farmed fish. Any meat at all. Any dairy at all. Any grains at all. Soya products. Trans fats. Any fats at all. Tomatoes. Aubergines. Any nightshade fruit at all.* It's called the Aunt Sonja Diet, but also owes a lot to the hundreds of American diet books her mother has at home. There are no other books in the house, just those. On the Aunt Sonja Diet there is, of course, to be no eating before lunchtime, except fruit. No dates. No bananas. Everyone loves Bovril and it only has 21 calories a cup, so that is allowed even though Bianca says it will give them all mad cow disease. In the Year 11 common room there is a job lot of Bovril that has been there since approximately 1988 and seems still to be edible. Bianca says 1988 was the pinnacle of mad cow disease, but no one has died yet.

The only sugar officially allowed on the diet is in Sherbet Fountains and the reason for this is that the sugar comes in paper, which makes it OK. Sherbet Fountains are wholesome because they are old-fashioned and, in the case of the ones in the village shop, long out of date and on special offer. Tash pretends she's read somewhere that calories evaporate from old or fermented products. Kimchi is allowed, not that Mrs Cuckoo has ever heard of kimchi. And sauerkraut. And the Bovril gets another tick as well because it is certainly aged. Liquorice is good for you, but no one actually likes the liquorice in Sherbet Fountains and so one day they put approximately twenty liquorice sticks in Bianca's cubby-hole, just for the hell of it.

The biology teacher is called Dr Morgan and he is a man. He is the only man who lives in the school

27

apart from the headmaster. He has the room next door to Sin-Jin's. His blond hair is slightly too long and prone to grease and he has grown a little blond beard like a Swedish pop star from the days of the Bovril. The teachers have their own corridor in Maids, the old servants' wing of the house. On the other side of Dr Morgan's room is Madame Vincent. Miss Annabel, the arthritic dance teacher, is down the corridor with Mrs Cuckoo. All the other teachers live in the village, or the local town, or Stevenage. The headmaster has his own house in the grounds by the lake where Princess Augusta drowned. He had a wife once, but not any more. Sometimes people say that she left him. Other times the rumour is that she died. There's an odd little grave in the school grounds that some people believe is hers. Once someone said that she was only twenty years old when she died, and extraordinarily thin, from a disease.

Today's biology lesson involves a video of a man who eats a miniature camera which then travels through his stomach recording the whole digestive process. It is literally the most gross thing anybody has ever seen.

For reasons unknown there is a painting of Princess Augusta in the biology lab. It looks wrong: dark oil paint set against the bright white walls. It appears not to have been chosen entirely randomly, however, as Princess Augusta is wearing a white dress that could be a nurse's uniform. Could Princess Augusta have administered aid to anybody? It seems unlikely. There wasn't even science back in the days of Princess Augusta, surely?

'Sir?' asks Lissa. 'Sir? Princess Augusta doesn't want to see all this poo, sir.'

'Girls, please.' Dr Morgan sighs. 'This is not "poo".'

'It's still really gross, though, Dr Morgan.'

'It is called chyme,' says Dr Morgan. 'It's not gross, girls. You all have it inside you right now. All those lovely bits of undigested food, your cornflakes or whatever you had for breakfast . . .'

'Bianca doesn't,' whispers someone. People giggle.

'What if you just eat fruit, sir?'

'Eating just fruit is very unhealthy. You need a balanced diet.'

On screen, the camera travels through a lot of stuff that looks like Sandwich Spread smeared on alien tentacles and then finally gets to the poo.

'I just can't believe you're actually showing us this, sir,' says Lissa.

'I'm going to complain to my father,' says Tiffanie.

Dr Morgan sighs and runs his hand through his scrawny beard.

*

It's a warm day in early October that reminds Tash of home. Something about the low depth of the heat. Its refulgent glow. The dining room has long windows at

29

the end that no one can see out of properly because they are too high, and covered with criss-cross bits of metal. Down the other wall are normal sash windows, one of which is open. A sleepy bumblebee has got in and is dancing towards the light, initially with hope, then with increasing frustration, because going up and following the light – both of which are hardwired if you are a bee – is not working. The bee cannot possibly know that to escape it will have to first go backwards, then downwards, towards darkness, and then double-back in a direction so completely against its nature and biology as to be unimaginable. But at the end of all that is the open window: the freedom that the bee has probably forgotten by now. The real light.

Natasha imagines someone explaining all this in a spiritual way. Like, how this is so similar to life. An old rabbi at a long-ago school says it. Then Dr Morgan. Mr Hendrix. She watches, willing the bee to just *go down*. She thinks it very hard, in Russian and then in English. Come this way, she thinks, just a little bit, and then—

Then Sin-Jin comes over with a paperback copy of the *General Prologue to the Canterbury Tales* and beats the bee to death.

*

Bianca has been sent to the headmaster again, and this time he has asked her to go to his house. The headmaster is known for coming up with 'improving' activities for naughty girls. Sometimes he reads them books, extremely boring books, often about Napoleon or Queen Victoria, or sometimes even self-published local history. Sometimes he gives them a younger girl to look after, although nowadays the younger girls and older girls are kept separate because of the recent crushlet-abuse incidents. Bianca wasn't involved in that, and apparently it really was just a few trips to the village shop, a bit of sewing and only a single episode where one girl locked another girl's crushlet in the haunted basement of the Dower House.

A crushlet is a younger girl who wants to be you. At best it's a creepy sort of mentoring. You get a letter in your cubby-hole with a heart sticker on the envelope, or a hand-drawn kitten, or something like that, declaring that a girl has a crush on you. No one wants to be Bianca. Or, at least, the only girls who would want to be Bianca are also the sort of girls who do not own stickers and cannot draw and hate kittens because they are cute, or only like them because they are so light and small.

As Bianca walks to the headmaster's house she imagines herself a fawn in the dark night, snow falling gently on her ruddy fur, and she thinks about Princess Augusta coming here to drown herself, and wonders if she meant to, or if she just thought she could swim. Was she trying to get the black diamond back? Because, really, what the fuck would you do once it was gone? It must be found, the black diamond. Only then will the light return. The pellucid, desperate light.

*

They go to Stevenage on a geography trip. What kind of geography trip takes you to what must be the worst town in the history of the universe, well, except for all those Soviet ruins, of course, and the towns near Chernobyl? Someone should nuke this one. At McDonald's they stop for diet drinks and kids' meals. There are boys; boys everywhere. These are worse than the VBs, surely? They wear clothes from Sports Direct that smell of cheap chemicals and their breath is all Special Sauce and bubblegum vape. Everyone, literally everyone, who lives in this town is fat. The only people who are not fat look like pleb versions of Bianca and have pushchairs full of children, long, stringy hair and thousands of piercings. The men all have ridiculous tattoos. These are not the sexy tattoos of pop stars and footballers but desperate cries for help rendered in fading ink. Luckily it's autumn, so not many of these can be seen. However, someone remembers the time the girls were taken to a local swimming baths near here and there were fat men with angel wings on their backs, and the names and birthdates of all their children. Tash and Tiffanie link arms because they are now best friends, and Danielle cries the soft tears of a day-girl with mild PMT.

32

What is the geography of Stevenage? No one knows. As well as the fat people, there are lots of roundabouts and a building site.

'Sir?' someone asks the teacher. Mr Hendrix is a Marxist Existentialist with a beard. No one knows how he came to be teaching at the school. 'Do you really live here? It's horrible.'

Mr Hendrix smiles. His beard is more authentic than Dr Morgan's. He has dark hair and is sexier in general. There is a rumour that he has a tattoo of his ex-girlfriend's name on his chest, but no one has ever seen it. Also the words *Fail Better* on his upper arm.

'Yes, I live here. What's wrong with that?'

'Oh my God, sir, it's full of plebs.'

'We don't use that word, Rachel. That's five house points you've just lost.'

No one, literally no one, gives a fuck about house points.

'What about *povvos*, sir, can we say that?'

'Absolutely not.'

'And so many fat people. Why are they all so fat, sir?'

'Because of capitalism, Lissa. Because of your fathers and what they do.'

'Sir, that's sexist! Some of our mothers might be capitalists too.'

The girls are given clipboards and sent off to interview locals about extremely boring things like jobs and housing. Geography is surely supposed to be about exotic places, animals, tribes and capital cities, not this shit. Geography should involve yachts at the very least. No one does it properly. It's cold, and everyone looks for warm places instead. McDonald's, department stores, Topshop.

Then Donya comes out of a department store with a free sample of a new moisturiser and suddenly everyone needs free samples and there is a rampage of these beskirted long-limbed exotic creatures with great bone structure. They stampede into Debenhams and BHS, both of which smell of bad cafeterias and children's nappies and wee. None of the shoppers know that the skirts are school policy, that you can't leave the school grounds without one on. Everyone must think that these girls have chosen, brazenly, to flaunt their legs, their perfect legs, with their expensive knees and beautiful freckles, most of which, thankfully, are hidden under tights: Boots cheapos for the English girls; pure merino for the others.

Tiffanie is wearing a short black leather garment that is against the rules in every possible way apart from the fact that it is a skirt. Lissa is in denim, also not allowed. Bianca is wearing a pink tutu. She's wearing it over leopard-print leggings, also not allowed. Is it an actual skirt? Or is it in fact one of her ballet outfits? Maybe from the show last year . . . ? Tash only has one skirt: a Halpern zebra-print sequined satin mini she got off Net-a-Porter for £990 with her black Amex when she realised she needed a skirt to be able to leave the school. She didn't mean to order something so expensive: she didn't understand the exchange rate. But no one seems to care. Danielle smuggles in the Net-a-Porter packages in return for small gifts: pink Converse; the odd silk scarf. Mr Hendrix can't do anything about the girls' choice of skirts. Like, exactly what the fuck is he supposed to do?

The coach is coming at six but Bianca is missing. Eventually the others find her in the basement of the local nightclub, watching with her big lake-blue eyes as the DJ practises his set for the night. The DJ is thin and black with a buzzcut and a t-shirt that says *Welcome to the Badlands*. He's playing a record by Azealia Banks and smoking a spliff. It is one of the most complicated and perplexing things the girls have ever seen. Especially now Bianca takes the spliff from the DJ and puffs on it, as if she's been doing this her whole life. Then she starts dancing, and it looks real, like something off the pop videos they sometimes watch on a Saturday morning at Danielle's house in the village. Like, no one knew Bianca could dance; well, not anything other than ballet. Her long arms flail about like spaghetti being thrown at a wall. Her tutu suddenly makes an odd sort of sense.

The DJ's friend comes in.

'More girls,' he says. 'Where you girls come from, den?' He's white, but talks like he isn't.

No one says anything. Everyone is blushing. Everyone is trying to make their limbs do something 'cool' but everyone just wants to run away giggling because their insides feel like wriggly worms and childish things. It's dark down here, and it smells smoky and sour. This isn't a place for children. The walls are lined in crushed black velvet that looks sort of pathetic in daylight, and also frightening. It's torn in places, and stained with splashes of beer. There's a locked cloakroom. A sticky floor. Hints of mucilage.

'Come on, Bianca,' says Lissa. 'The coach is here.'

'*The coach is here*,' repeats the white boy, mimicking Lissa's accent, making it sound more like *the couch is hair*. 'Where de fuck you girls from, den? You posh girls?'

No one says anything.

'You posh girls want some spliff?' he says. 'That what you here for?'

Of course they want some. No one has ever tried drugs before, and now here they are and some skinny pleb is offering it for free. No one is scared. No one's ever died from smoking spliffs, right? Anyway, there are only two boys and there are five of them even if you don't count Bianca. If something went wrong, they could . . . What? But no one thinks of that anyway. Natasha remembers what Aunt Sonja said, though, and only pretends to inhale when it's her turn. She has the Russian Deep Heat, just in case.

By the time the girls get back to the coach they are in big trouble. Especially as they are even later after stopping to sign autographs on the way back. Why not? That guy in Starbucks thought they were an actual girl band, which was the most hilarious thing ever.

'That's another ten house points gone,' says Mr Hendrix.

'Sir?' says Elle, the captain of the hockey team. 'Sir, they're not all in the same house.'

'A plague on both your houses,' says Bianca, and starts giggling.

The others manoeuvre her to the back of the coach.

Mr Hendrix sighs and puts Bob Dylan on the coach stereo system and all the girls groan because they mistakenly think Bob Dylan is wholesome and a hippy and an anti-capitalist. The only one who likes it is Donya, who has a badly-hidden crush on Mr Hendrix.

'Sir,' she says, as the coach sets off in the dark, cold evening.

'Yes, Donya?'

'Are you related to Jimi Hendrix, sir?'

'Yes, Donya.'

'Are you really, though, sir?'

'What do you think?'

*

The Year 11 common room is cleared out to be painted and someone finds a slam book from 1988 hidden behind the Bovril. Lots of faded photographs of thin girls with

37

weird flicky hairstyles pasted with actual glue next to fountain-penned lists of Things about Themselves: their favourite colours, bands, nicknames and so on. It's surprisingly dull, except for an old piece of paper that falls out that explains how to make friendship bracelets, which is of interest to Danielle, who likes making cute retro things. The second half of the book has been completed by boys at the Harrow School in London. They have pasted in photographs of themselves and song lyrics they like, often by Van Morrison, their career aspirations, their favourite animals (mostly snakes) and their 'ideal woman'. Vanessa Paradis features a lot. There are pictures of her in a yellow sweatshirt and boyfriend jeans looking quite fat by today's standards. Probably over eight stone.

Donya insists on taking the slam book to history class.

'It's a kind of history,' she says. 'It's like folk history or something.'

'*Vestiges archéologiques*,' says Tiffanie.

Mr Hendrix agrees about folk history, which is how the girls have come to be creating a new slam book that they are going to send to the boys who are at Harrow now. Turns out that Mr Hendrix, for all his Marxist Existentialism, actually went to Harrow, and so he is going to set it up with the history teacher there. And Bianca's twin brother goes there too. No one knew Bianca even had a twin brother, and she might even be lying:

you never know. Anyway, everyone will re-enact the 1980s by producing new slam books and sending them through the actual post.

'Sir?' says Rachel. 'Princess Augusta never had to glue her photograph in what is essentially a catalogue for—'

'A sex catalogue,' says Bianca, darkly. The photograph she has chosen to put into the slam book makes her look like a praying mantis in shadow. Her massive eyes perch atop a long, dark line that might be wearing a black dress and standing against a black wall.

'This is basically organised prostitution,' agrees Lissa.

'*Catalogue de sexe*,' says Tiffanie, with a sparkle in her eyes. Does she make this stuff up, or is it actual French? No one knows. Madame Vincent does not talk about anything to do with *sexe*. Is *sexe* French for sex? It seems too easy somehow. Too lazy.

'Girls,' says Mr Hendrix. 'If you had any house points left I'd be taking them away. What's wrong with you? This is your chance to experience history as it is lived.'

'Can't we just go on the internet, sir?'

'It's not the same, girls. You know that. Now, let's think of some contemporary touches we can add. Who wants to suggest something?'

In the end they all add their real mobile numbers to their profiles, except for Bianca, who makes one up.

*

39

Behind the Bovril also lurked a calorie-counter from the olden days before the internet. It's a little paperback with tiny writing and pink and brown stains that might be jam and Bovril but also might not be. It gets passed around during prep when Sin-Jin is asleep. The game is this: find the grossest, most calorific meal you can. Is it fondue? (What even is that?) Fondue with chips. Fondue with chips and beans and Thousand Island dressing and trifle. And pie. Lots and lots of pie. With mash, made with a whole packet of butter and several large tablespoons of double cream. Double cream dripping off the spoon and down the sides of the plate and on the floor. People treading in the double cream and slipping on it and dying.

The game was Bianca's idea.

Bianca's last game involved finding pictures of the celebrities with the fattest arms. The one before that was collecting screenshots of obese children from Instagram. There was also the Fat Ballerina Challenge, where you had to find images of professional dancers and zoom in on their arses or their stomachs or their chins and rank the most gross body parts in order.

Later, in bed, Tash gets out her silver phone and looks on the Weight Watchers site. In a day you are supposed to eat 23 points' worth of food. She browses the restaurant possibilities. She's hardly eaten Indian food in her life, thank God, because Indian Restaurant Chicken Tikka Masala is 81 points. The very thought is dizzying. If you added pilau rice (20), naan (28) and a couple of onion bhajis (18) that would be 147 points. Almost a whole week's worth of points in one meal. Without pudding or anything.

Tash lies about her age and her height and signs up.

*

Tiffanie walks around the dorm with her tits out literally all the time, so Tash and Lissa have started doing it too. Tiffanie's tits are little works of art, or possibly craft: two perfect upside-down teacups. They are brown, with rose-coloured nipples that always point upwards.

It's a Tuesday evening a few weeks before they break up for Christmas. Everyone's talking about the Cambridge trip the following Saturday, and then the disco where there will be no boys, of course, but at least the girls will be allowed to choose the music. Everyone is into Azealia Banks right now after the episode in Stevenage, although a rumour is going around that the teachers are going to delete anything with an E from the playlist. It's almost nine o'clock. Everyone's chilling out before bedtime. Lissa is putting all her underwear in a toggle bag for laundry day tomorrow. She's putting dark and light things together, because she doesn't care. Tash is reading French *Vogue* with her headphones in. Then Bianca appears from one of the bathrooms fully clothed and with her school cape on. Bianca never shows more of her body than is absolutely necessary. She is always in clothes. She even

41

sleeps fully dressed in her strange white pyjamas. But she doesn't normally wear her cape inside.

'Where are you go-*ange?*' says Tiffanie.

Tiffanie has been in the UK for almost five years but her French accent is as thick as it was when she arrived. She is too lazy, too French and frankly too fucking cool to learn English pronunciation and so she says all words as if they were French. So going becomes go-*ange*, the last bit said a little like the *anj* in *banjo*. And the *where* and the *are* are simply two long growls.

'Yeah, what are you doing?' says Tash. She has taken to doing it too, as have some of the English girls. Doo-*ange*. What are you doo-*ange?* The Rs are always extravagantly rolled as well, even in English words.

'Headmaster's house,' says Bianca.

'Again?' says Lissa. 'That's weird. What have you done this time?'

Bianca shrugs like a little bird that can't yet fly, or a moth whose wings are still covered in weird gleim and other crap from its cocoon.

'Oui, what have you done, Océane?'

Océane is French for Hannah. Manon is French for Emily. Or maybe it's the other way around. In any case, the English concept of Hannah and Emily – the most popular names for plebs in the year they were all born; in the olden days known as Sharon and Tracey – is translated into French as Océane and Manon. In Russian the old-fashioned versions are Lyudmila and Ninel.

42

Natasha's mother is called Lyudmila. Tash struggles to think what other girls of her age are called. Like, she's kind of forgotten already.

'I said "fuck" to Miss Annabel. I sort of told her to fuck off.'

'Pourquoi?'

'Parce que . . . because she said I'm too thin for ballet.' Bianca sighs. 'Like that's even possible. But it's not my fault I'm thin. I eat literally all the time.'

'I thought you were amazing at ballet?'

It's true. Bianca's too good to even take classes with the other girls. She shrugs again, and scurries off into the cold night like something from a fairy tale.

After that, Rachel comes in from next door and gets everyone to come and look at the massive turd that is in one of the toilets. It's the largest poo anyone has ever seen. No one even has a dog capable of doing such a massive shit. It's shaped like a nuclear submarine. It's unclear whether Rachel has done this herself, or whether it was deposited by someone else.

'Bianca?' asks someone.

'That would not fit in Bianca,' says Lissa.

Someone flushes the toilet, but the poo remains.

*

Everyone's making friendship bracelets. Sin-Jin buys the embroidery thread at the haberdasher's in Stevenage.

Here's how you do it: you pick three attractive colours and cut two long pieces of thread for each one. Then you knot them all together and use a safety pin to—

'Girls,' says Sin-Jin. 'Girls, DON'T put safety pins in your tights. I've told you before.'

For days now they've been going around with bits of coloured embroidery thread hanging from their tights or their skirts. It is in this state that they are called into the headmaster's study: Tash, Tiffanie, Rachel, Lissa, Danielle and Donya.

'Well,' says Sin-Jin. 'There's no time to take them off now. And I don't think Dr Moone is going to be worried about that today. Come on. Quickly.'

There is nowhere for them to sit, so they all stand in front of the massive mahogany desk with bits of thread dangling down their legs like the insides of abandoned toys. Dark pictures hang on the wooden panels that line the study. None of them are of Princess Augusta. They are all men, or horses.

Dr Moone is one of those old important people that looks exactly like other old important people. His body is a sack filled with dead kittens and his skin is a dusty wooden antique. When he walks, it is with an exaggerated limp because of having once caught his leg in a rat trap in whatever colonial backwater his father was stationed in. He is basically a different species: one that should be respected and revered and—

He breathes in. 'Good morning, girls.' There's a

44

complicated pause. He looks pained, or, at least, like someone who has just decided to adopt a pained look. 'What I'm about to tell you is confidential. You won't be able to talk to the other girls about it, do you understand? What we're about to discuss has to stay in this room.'

Serious nods. Of course, sir. Anything you say. Aunt Sonja would not agree to something on these terms, but Aunt Sonja is not here. Also, Aunt Sonja may have forgotten what it's like to be fifteen and entrusted with a secret by your actual headmaster.

Dr Moone sighs long and hard like a plane landing. The plane comes to a halt.

'Bianca is dead,' he says. He says it without emotion.

Tash wants to laugh. She can feel the prickle coming off the other girls as well. They all want to laugh and laugh and—

Wait, no. In fact, Donya has fainted. Sin-Jin is wafting something over her that might be a paperback copy of the *General Prologue to the Canterbury Tales*. It might even be the copy with the bits of dead bee on it. Now she is calling sick bay. Everyone else stands there trying to seem grown-up enough to be able to take this news without laughing or fainting. Is there any other possible reaction? Tash feels oddly excited, like standing on the edge of a high diving board. She can feel her actual blood pumping around her actual body and she sways, gulps, but does not faint. No one knows what to do. Who is going to be the first to cry? Are they expected to cry? If they cry over something that is essentially a secret, will other people find out? But if they don't cry over their friend who is dead, then—

'I understand that you were her special friends,' says Dr Moone. 'As well as the fact that some of you shared a dorm with her. This is why you are being told first. Now, I have to ask you a very serious question. Why do you think she died?'

Sin-Jin shoots him a strange look then. It's almost imperceptible.

No one ever talks back to Dr Moone. If this was Dr Morgan or Mr Hendrix, they would be asking all sorts of inappropriate questions right now. Where was she found? When did it happen? OK – those are appropriate questions, but on hearing she was found in the lake perhaps they would ask if she had been partially eaten by fish, and enquire whether or not she floated, and whether the VBs were involved and what Princess Augusta would think about it all. Perhaps. *Perhaps.*

No one says anything.

'You all spend a lot of time on diets, I hear.'

Everyone looks at the floor.

'We've read Bianca's diary. There are going to be a lot of changes in the next few weeks. I expect you to co-operate with them.'

Everyone nods.

'Sir?' says Rachel. 'What do we say when people ask where Bianca is?'

'She's been suspended,' he says. 'For leading you all astray. For encouraging you to diet too much.'

Sin-Jin gives him the look again.

If this were a different teacher the girls would definitely argue. Objectively it is a stupid idea, with the potential for maximum trauma. What's going to happen when everyone finds out that these six girls were able to lie about something so grave? Will this enhance their future prospects or not? Is this something that they can put on university applications? *Ability to lie about something really, really serious.* No one is sure. Something isn't right about this.

'I am going to discuss it with the other senior staff,' says Dr Moone. 'But at the moment that is what we have decided to do. You can talk among yourselves. We know you'll want to do that. Your dorms are away from the others, so whenever you want to go there in the day you can. But you need to promise that you will not tell anyone for now. Not even your parents.'

Silence.

'Do you promise?'

'Yes, sir.'

*

Danielle takes Bianca's bed. It doesn't quite fit with the suspension story: after all, how normal is it for one girl to be suspended and then have her things boxed up and

47

put into storage while another girl moves in? *Maybe*, whisper the other girls, *maybe Bianca's been expelled*. That becomes the official unofficial story, even though the fake suspension hasn't even been announced. Danielle's been on some sort of waiting list, apparently. Her parents are splitting up and selling the house in the village. Her mother is moving to London and her father is relocating to Dubai. Danielle lies in Bianca's bed crying and listening to *Lemonade* and making a friendship bracelet with only black embroidery thread. The pattern looks lovely, even though the colour is the same all the way through. But then Danielle is talented like that.

The other girls flutter around like pages torn from a forbidden book and no one makes jokes about poo or Princess Augusta. They don't cry in case someone sees them. They are taking their secret very, very seriously. Occasionally they look at each other and say, 'My God.' If they do need to cry they lock themselves in one of the bathrooms and run all the taps.

On Monday, and without warning, Dr Moone comes into the dining hall at breakfast and announces to everyone that Bianca is dead.

*

There is talk of cancelling the Cambridge trip and the disco, but then someone has the idea that it should be turned into sort of a wake for Bianca. The funeral is going to be the following Monday in London but Bianca's parents have requested that no one from the school attends. So the wake would be something they could do instead; it would be a chance to celebrate her life. Dance to Azealia Banks and Ariana Grande and . . .

'You're so morbid,' says Becky with the bad hair.

Becky with the bad hair is filling in her application to become Head Girl. You need two references and an amazing personal statement. It helps if you've been in sports teams, got drama qualifications, done your maths exams early. Perhaps being really tall helps? The deadline is after Christmas. The Head Girl only changes every two years – biannually, or biennially, one of those – because you do it for the whole of Years 12 and 13. The Head Girl spends a lot of time with Dr Moone and the senior staff helping to run the school. The current Head Girl is called Thérèse. She is very thin and has long stringy blonde hair, a bit like . . . Wait, wasn't she Bianca's crush all those years ago? That's right, someone says, Bianca was her *crushlet*.

While the others make plans to go and see Thérèse, who has a minimalist study-bedroom in Maids quite near the teachers' corridor, and is remotely related to Tiffanie in some French aristocratic way no one understands, Natasha wonders whether she should apply to be Head Girl. It was the way the headmaster spoke to them about Bianca. And OK, so he lied about it being a secret, and lied about them being trusted and special, but Tash is attracted to his gravitas. She wants teachers to speak to her like that again.

And no one wants Becky with the bad hair to be Head Girl. Becky with the bad hair is already becoming something of a menace. She has started an Anti Ana group with her friends Bella and Elle, presumably because of the rumours that Bianca was in a Pro Ana group. It's yet another way of obsessing about food, and an excuse to look at all the disgusting Pinterest boards about Thinspiration, and guides on how to fast without fainting, but she has presented it to the teachers in a way that seems wholesome and healthy. She is tasked with doing a survey and some interviews to find out about the attitude of girls in the school to food and dieting. Literally everyone lies. The girls who regularly have two slices of treacle tart don't admit to ever having any. The girls who hide their treacle tart say they eat it all the time. Baffling statistics are produced. It seems that dieting makes you fat! And eating all the time makes you thin. Who knew?

But worse: 90 per cent of the school has some sort of eating disorder.

'Right,' says Dr Moone. 'Time for action.'

*

The eating-disorder men look like criminals. They are called Tony and Dominic. They are from Scotland. Tony

50

has a shaved head and wears utility clothes with walking boots. It's like normcore but real. Like he's just been released from prison. Dominic has shifty eyes. He wears black Converse because he's trying to be young. He wears them with skinny black jeans and a black t-shirt. Tony and Dominic must be in their late forties, or even older. Everyone tries to find something sexy about them but there is literally nothing, which is a shame because everyone is bored of Mr Hendrix, and no one fancies Dr Morgan except for Becky with the bad hair. His breath is just—

'Right. We're not going to start with good morning and all that crap,' says Dominic. 'This shit is real.'

Sin-Jin sighs loudly and side-eyes Madame Vincent.

Becky with the bad hair moves her chair slightly closer. These are the orange bucket chairs from the drama studio that give everyone terrible static in the winter and sticky legs in the summer. But they are lightweight and they stack well, which is why someone ordered hundreds of them. They will never wear out. The same kinds of things could be said of the eating-disorder men. Someone's ordered them from somewhere, but how? Like, where do you even get two therapists who look so much like paedophiles?

The internet, of course.

'You are all here because you have problems with food,' says Tony. He pronounces this *fut*. It sounds a bit like *foot*. It's also a little like he's spitting. He does look quite

51

angry. Why? They're not his daughters. Why does he even care?

'We're going to begin by talking about some of the difficulties you have had with fut,' says Dominic. 'Tony will lead you through this section and then I'm going to teach you a little bit of EFT tapping at the end. After that, I hope you'll be cured of your issues with fut once and for all.'

'OK,' says Tony. 'I want you all to shut your eyes. Now, I need you to think of the worst thing that's ever happened with you and fut. It might be that time you ate a whole trifle and then vomited it up. It might be when you decided to eat only raw fut and became so weak you could not leave the house. Maybe you did a juice fast and got explosive diarrhoea? Nothing is too bad or too disgusting for us. We just want to hear your real stories. This is going to be difficult for some of youse, I know, but it's necessary. We have to get real, here. Really, really real.'

Everyone thinks, and sighs, and tries to touch the metal bits of their chairs to discharge some of the static. You can almost hear it crackling through the room. Tiffanie has discovered that she can make Becky's bad hair stand on end by just raising her palms up behind it and—

'OK,' says Tony. 'Who's got something to share? You.' He points at Flick, a usually quiet girl with freckles and plump cheeks. Why has Flick got her hand up for this?

'It was during the Easter holidays,' says Flick. 'There's

this YouTube channel with this American girl on it who tries out these different diets? This particular week she was doing one of the Victoria's Secret Model Challenges. There are loads. Anyway, I tried to copy her but I literally couldn't even make it through the first five minutes of the workout. Then my sister bought a bag of ten doughnuts and ate one and then left them in the kitchen. I basically ate nine doughnuts while watching the rest of this one YouTube video. Like, I'm literally sitting there watching her do a butt workout while I'm stuffing my face. Afterwards I thought about killing myself.'

'Right, good,' says Tony. 'And if you had to mark that experience out of ten, with one being OK and ten being the worst experience possible, what would it be?'

'A nine,' says Flick.

'What would have made it a ten?'

'Well, I guess if I *had* killed myself?'

'Good,' says Tony. 'Who's next?'

Bella puts her hand up. 'My periods stopped because of all the sport, and because I didn't eat enough.' Bella is vice-captain of the hockey team. All that bending over swiping at weeds with a long stick must be exhausting, but—

'Her period has not even started,' whispers Tiffanie loudly. Tash giggles and Dominic glares at her. He has the eyes of a lifeguard who lets people drown.

'And what number would you give that?' Tony asks.

'Nine as well,' says Bella.

'And can you think of a particular scene that would illustrate how bad this made you feel?'

'I don't know. I guess there was one day I thought I had got my period and everything was normal again and I inserted a tampon and eight hours later when it was time to take it out I couldn't get it out and I had to go to the school nurse to help me and basically I know this is gross but it wouldn't come out because it was so dry, because there was no blood, and I didn't have another period for maybe a year?'

The sharing goes on. If Bianca were here . . . But she's not. But if she were, she would have real stories, not that she would ever tell anyone about them. This stuff is just a combination of dull, non-eating-disorder anecdotes and urban myths and the usual teenage crap. When it's Natasha's turn she doesn't know where to start. There are so many things, but do any of them make her feel anything? Like, does she actually care? It's her mother who has a problem with food, anyway, not her.

'I threw away a box of chocolates,' she says in the end, with a shrug. She doesn't say that these were her parting gift from Nico. That she loved him so much less because of it. That she hasn't replied to his last letter. That he bought her vegan chocolates even though she is not a vegan and he is not a vegan but probably because he's a guy and didn't read the label properly. That he does not know about her father, and everything that has happened. 'Just before I flew here from Moscow.'

'And how did that make you feel?' says Tony.

Tash shrugs again. 'I don't know,' she says.

'Bad?' prompts Tony.

'Sure,' says Tash. 'Yeah. I wished I hadn't done it.'

'On a scale of one to ten?'

'Like a four?'

'A four. A *four*.' He starts pacing. 'Are you sure?'

'I don't know.'

'How many of the chocolates did you eat?'

'One.'

'Really? Are you sure it wasn't the whole box?'

'Um . . .'

'You ate the whole box because you're a disgusting fat bitch.'

Tash looks at Tiffanie, who has arranged her finger and thumb in an L on her forehead, which is pointing towards Tony. Tash wants to laugh but she can't.

'Right?' says Tony.

'No,' says Tiffanie. 'Because she is not *anorexique*.'

'I ate one,' says Tash. 'Then I threw the box away because I was about to get on a plane and I didn't want to be tempted.'

'Aha! *Tempted*. Why would you say that?'

'Because I'm normal. I would have been bored on the plane and eaten something I didn't want to eat, so I threw them away so I couldn't.'

Tony sighs. 'Right, well, you can sit out of the next part, then, if you're so "normal".'

For the next fifteen minutes Tony gets everyone to relive their nine or ten experience, first the way it actually happens in their memory, then in black and white, then in third person. He makes them do it again and again and again.

Later on, in the dorm, the game is to make Tiffanie say *neuro-linguistic programming*, which is hilarious, especially as Tiffanie, who is topless as usual, insists on saying *langoustine* instead of *linguistic*, which takes the girls' minds off what happened with Tony and Dominic at the end, and the fact that it was their fault. The static had built up and up, and Elle was crying while reliving an experience when a boy saw her with something caught between her teeth, and Sin-Jin was whispering something to Madame Vincent, and Tash leant down to discharge the static on the leg of her chair but this time it made a cracking noise and made a spark and it actually *hurt*, so she said *Ow*, and then Tiffanie giggled and then—

'You think this is *funny*, do you?' said Dominic, glaring at them. 'You think this is a big *fucking laugh*, do you? You think anorexia is funny? Your friend has just *died*, and we are here trying to save your lives. Your actual *lives*.'

Silence.

'Even if you don't die of anorexia itself,' said Dominic, 'from your body actually eating itself and then stopping, because you have *killed* it, there are plenty of other ways to die along the way. Plenty. Have you ever seen a sex

56

slave being fed to a tiger? It's not fucking pretty, I can tell you. Fat girls don't get fed to tigers, they—'

It was at this point that Tiffanie and Tash and Lissa and Rachel and Danielle and even Donya pretty much lost it. Fat girls don't get fed to tigers??? WTF? They laughed until they cried, until they literally fell off their orange chairs in an explosion of static and grief and absurdity.

And then they got sent to the headmaster.

*

Tiffanie's Frenchness is like a massive planet with its own gravitational pull. If you want to have a good conversation with her, you have to speak French almost fluently. Everyone is therefore on course for an A* in French, except for Tiffanie herself, who does not understand the English instructions on the exam papers. You'd think Madame Vincent would be pleased with this but she is not. She despises these girls with their hipbones and collarbones and rolled-up skirts. She hates it when they laugh. She hates their teeth.

She volunteers to oversee their early morning punishments. She turns up at their dorms at 5.15 a.m., she's glad to, and she marches them out to the swimming pool for fifty laps before breakfast. They are not allowed towels. They look at each other's fat through scratched goggles in the milky waterlight. They have cold showers. Before prep in the evening they have to complete the three-mile cross-country route into the village and back. It's dark and they trip over tree roots and get old cobwebs in their hair and no one cares. Princess Augusta presumably never had to go on long runs, but no one talks about Princess Augusta any more.

While the girls swim, Madame Vincent does little squats, just little ones because of her knees, and when they run she does feeble press-ups, with her palms on the cold concrete by the swimming pool. Even though she is now fifty-six and a housemistress in the middle of nowhere, she is still French, and she still dreams of young, virile lovers. Lovers unlike Dr Morgan, who occasionally stumbles into her room after a long, lonely Sunday. She despises Tiffanie so much more than the other girls, because Tiffanie is French but will never become like her. Tiffanie will always have golden skin and rose-coloured nipples. Always.

*

Half-term. Natasha packs an overnight bag, puts on her Halpern skirt and takes the train to Kings Cross, where she is picked up by a pre-booked black cab.

It's Friday night and London is a massive jewel sparkling in the rain. So much money and beauty and light all concentrated in one place. Every street with billions of pounds' worth of clothes and perfumes and flesh, and ideas that exist, and ideas that almost exist, and ideas that do not exist yet. Miles and miles of blockchains. Blockchains all the way to the moon. Money, codes, hungry tigers. Steam on the windows. Small creatures hiding in dark spaces in basement car parks. The distinct species of mosquito that only exists on the London Underground hibernating, or whatever they do at this time of year. The deliquescence of early winter coats. Sneakbills and scrags in their puffa jackets and high-heeled ankle boots.

Aunt Sonja has a flat that looks over the Thames, with old river barges and party boats and ferries going past. The Thames reflects the jewel. Gives it fluorescence, and dignity. They need each other, the Thames and its jewel. They yearn for each other in the dark light, always.

Planes circle Essex and then queue up to land at Heathrow. They are also full of money. Money and biology and love. Is there anything else? One of the planes contains, apart from the pilot and co-pilot, only a single white Persian cat. Another contains a butler and some sushi. The jet trails of the planes break up and fall from the sky like scattering pearls, like the petals of white roses, like dustings of icing sugar, froth in the vapour.

In the kitchen, Aunt Sonja is explaining to Tash an algorithm her young colleague has developed which tells you what communication method someone is likely to use to do something secret like buy drugs or have an affair or groom an unwitting teenager. You take the person's birthdate, birthplace and gender and then put in a few facts, mainly about their clothes. Do they wear jeans? High heels? Men over fifty who don't wear jeans will use email. If they are over seventy they will write a note. But men between forty-two and forty-five who do wear jeans will use Snapchat. Tash imagines Tony and Dominic on Snapchat. The image is creepy but real. Normcore.

This is only if someone doesn't use social media, of course, Aunt Sonja says. If they use social media, then you can find out everything about them anyway. Literally anyone can find out literally anything from a social media account. Habits, movements, passwords: the lot. She is drinking champagne in a thin elegant glass and making dinner. It's brown rice and poached fish, with papaya and pineapple fruit salad to follow.

But this is old, she says. Blockchains are new. Well, they are old too, really.

There is a catalogue on the glass coffee table. Its text is in Russian, but it has images of London on the front: the Shard, the Gherkin, the Tower of London. Inside, there are images of bulletproof security cameras, and fingerprint entry-systems for apartments and offices. Gate systems for mansions and castles. Interiors of a country estate in Surrey. Prices.

Later, when Aunt Sonja has had several more glasses of champagne, she sits on the white sofa next to Tash and starts talking in Russian.

'Keep your beauty,' she says. 'Do everything you can to keep your beauty. But also care for your fragile soul.'

Natasha has noticed on this visit that Aunt Sonja is not, herself, beautiful. She is thin, but in a sad way. Her collarbones look sharp, not attractive. They jut. She is well-groomed and well-maintained, but she looks like money rather than sex or love. It's not that Natasha could put this into words, but she suddenly sees it, just as Aunt Sonja starts talking incoherently about nightclubs and dark-haired men and male prostitutes and something that happened last Friday night that Tash can't quite get a handle on. Someone called Reuben.

'Make men want you for *you*,' she says. 'Not your money.'

'I don't have any money,' says Tash, laughing a little nervously.

'Oh, you do. You will. It's a fucking disaster, by the way, having money, but you won't be able to escape it, not now your father's found you.'

'*Found* me? I—'

'He's going to try to marry you off to the son of one of his associates. Beauty will make sure you get a choice. Do you understand? If more than one person wants you, it means you have a choice.'

'What if I don't want to get married?'

'Then we'll need another plan.'

For the rest of half-term Aunt Sonja works long hours and Tash spends her days on the Underground. She

61

doesn't know where to get off, or what to do. She goes up and down on the Piccadilly Line because she likes the colour. She goes all the way to Heathrow Terminal 5 and gets off there and buys a coffee in the Departures terminal as if she were about to go somewhere else, maybe even home. She's been to Terminal 5 before, and it feels like a safe place. More than home, which she finds she can't remember. Is it sort of brown? Maybe it's actually black and white like in neuro-linguistic programming. Maybe it's third-person. Maybe it's simply gone. Two sagging sofas with covers that fall off and a cat with black hairs that stick to you.

She likes the fountain at Terminal 5. Tash imagines terrorists everywhere, imagines the hot flames of a sudden bomb, the cold steel of a machete, the silence between the bullets in a machine-gun attack in a crowded place, but she doesn't care. She likes jumping onto a Tube just before the doors close, pushing her body into the warm mass of commuters, tourists, real Londoners. Between Leicester Square and Covent Garden one afternoon she watches as a drop of another girl's sweat falls onto her arm. She feels, just once, a stranger's hand start to rub between her legs and she doesn't know what is happening at first because her jeans are quite thick and then he gets off and she wonders if she should have stopped him.

*

62

The next guest on the programme, which is now called 'Speak Out Against Eating Disorders', is called Anastasia. She is a recovering anorexic with her own YouTube channel and a respectable, but not jaw-dropping, 50k followers on Instagram. She is launching a gluten-free cookbook, and arrives by taxi with a skinny guy carrying boxes of these books that the school has pre-ordered and paid for. One for each girl.

The talk is in the freshly painted common room. There are to be no orange bucket chairs this time. Everyone squeezes onto sofas and beanbags and floor cushions and it's a bit like morning registration, except that instead of Sin-Jin recording their presence on her tablet, there is this entity, this tattooed outsider wearing leopard-skin platforms and swaying like a baby giraffe by the computers in the corner. She has a takeaway coffee cup even though there is literally nowhere to buy takeaway coffee between here and Stevenage. Where on earth has it come from? She clings to it as if it is a drip or an oxygen canister that she must have with her at all times. She sips from it. What's inside? It's unfathomable.

The skinny guy has gone somewhere, which is a shame because everyone wanted a good look at him. Why don't they have a car? Is Anastasia a pleb? The school can't have booked an actual pleb to come and talk to them, could it? Tash is fascinated. She has not yet quite learned how to spot what the others call a pleb in this country. But she knows that they are people like Nico. Like his mother. Like Tash, before her father found her and gave her a plastic bag full of money and a copy of Russian *Vogue*. Plebs' voices all the time through the walls of her mother's apartment, screaming at each other. The dull thumps of marriage and babies and the middle of the month.

'So hi, I guess,' is how Anastasia starts, and her voice is reassuringly that of an ex-private schoolgirl, albeit one who has embraced a different aesthetic entirely. She looks like a rock star, with her tattoos and multiple necklaces. One of the necklaces has her name on it in gold letters. Well, a shortened version of her name. In fact, it says *Ana*, which is troubling. Another is simply a triangle. Another is a series of gold hippos interspersed with gold hearts. The necklaces are perfectly layered.

It's like watching a YouTube video, like they used to do at Danielle's house on a Saturday morning before Dani's parents split up. Tash still watches YouTube videos sometimes on her silver phone, although they usually bore her. Girls with long hair and too much mascara going on and on about their 'goals' and their challenges and their breakups and their issues and exactly what they eat in a day. But the videos are useful for picking up English expressions. At the moment Tash's French is improving faster than her English, which wasn't the point at all. But her English is pretty good: it always was. Professor Dimitrov always said she had a special talent for languages. And her mother's boyfriends always spoke English.

Anastasia sips again from her takeaway coffee cup. She has her long blonde hair up in a high scruffy ponytail. Her gold hoop earrings bob as she speaks. She has a helix piercing as well: a tiny silver sleeper with a diamond heart dangling from it. She's wearing ripped jeans, which are not allowed in the school, and which give her appearance an extra thrill. And of course there's the fact that she has a navel piercing, and a cropped t-shirt to show it off. And an oversize cropped hoodie. So many school rules broken all at the same time. It's beautiful.

'So I'm here to talk to you about food issues,' she says, in her well-educated voice. 'And tell you about my anorexia journey, and some of the mistakes I made that I hope you won't make.' When she smiles, her whole face sort of scrunches. She's all softness and innocence, except for her collarbones, which reach out more sharply and more desperately even than Aunt Sonja's do. Her arms are like beautiful slender branches from a silver birch tree. She has a lot of bangles, as well as a couple of festival bands. The word *Always* is tattooed on her left forearm in black courier. With a bit less mascara, this is how everyone would want to look, if an angel came and gave them a choice. Maybe even the mascara is not as bad as it first seemed. It makes Anastasia seem extra-terrestrial, and kind of meta.

'I was weighing myself like five times a day,' she's saying. 'I counted the calories of everything I ate, obsessively. I'd go down to like 500 calories a day and I'd hate

65

myself if I even ate a banana. I mean, bananas are a bit gross anyway, because they contain like 27 grams of carbs just in a single one, but I'd even feel guilty if I ate an apple. I mean, again, it's like 14 grams of carbs, which is a third of what I'd be trying to have. You know that you need to be having less than 50 grams of carbs a day for serious fat loss?' She laughs. 'God, I'm so full of those bullshit stats. It's like they never leave you. And the mantras? *Hunger is just weakness leaving the body*, for example. *Nothing tastes as good as skinny feels.* You'll need to ditch those as soon as you can. And learn that 75 grams of carbs a day is the right amount, not 50.'

Anastasia sips once more from the takeaway coffee cup. Whatever is in there must be so cold. Maybe it's even a frappé, but don't those come in clear plastic?

'Recently,' she says, 'I realised I still had some food issues. Like, even if you think you've beaten anorexia it's actually still there? For example, I have not eaten ice cream since I was nine years old. It was when I was ten that I stopped eating and my parents had me diagnosed as anorexic. So I basically haven't eaten ice cream since then. The other day I made a list of things I won't eat that are like food fears I still have to overcome? Burgers with cheese. I mean, who doesn't have cheese on their burger? Uh, me! Still! And milk in coffee. I always saw milk in coffee as just bad calories, like a disgusting white poop of fat and bacteria and cow pus? So that's on my list too. I have never eaten a chip! Like, I got in the habit of always choosing the least calorific thing in the shop? So in most places it's basically a salad, no dressing. Sometimes a fruit salad. Sometimes miso soup. I see you have a lot of Bovril here? That's a good choice for weight loss. But obviously I should now be choosing hot chocolate instead. With whipped cream and marshmallows. Like, I have to be comfortable with these things, I know I do, but I'm just not? A pizza. A whole pizza with a stuffed crust. And salad dressing. Like we have all been conditioned to never even have salad dressing. But who wants dry salad? We have to learn to live a little, ladies.'

Year 11 is transfixed. The form's three fat girls, Rachel, Zoe and Ayesha, shift uncomfortably. Rachel's legs have stuck together as usual; the others' probably have too. The fat girls are not on floor cushions or beanbags, because getting up in public from any kind of low furniture is so embarrassing. Anastasia's forbidden foods are basically their go-to staples. Double chocolate cookies. Cakes made of traditional ingredients rather than the raw vegan gluten-free ones assembled with grated beetroot. Actual Coke rather than Coke Zero. Isn't Anastasia afraid of turning out like the fat girls, with their lumps and rolls and hair and zits and bad posture caused by trying to hide from life? Obviously, which is why this is a list and not a reality. To be Anastasia you have to put these items on a list but never in your actual mouth. You have to talk about food all the time but never, ever eat it.

If this is the face of anorexia, pretty much everyone wants in.

To end her talk, Anastasia brings up Instagram on the big screen and shows the girls how to search for anorexia hashtags like #thinspo and #thinspiration and #bonespo and #anathinspo and #thin and #skinny and #ana and #thighgap. When she puts #thighgap into the search box, Instagram comes up with a message: *Posts with words or tags you're searching for often encourage behavior that can cause harm and even lead to death. If you're going through something difficult, we'd like to help.*

'Yeah, so all the anorexic girls obviously just ignore that warning,' says Anastasia. 'And of course it's not like anyone really cares, right? I mean, they let the hashtags exist. Anyway, I apologise if what follows is a bit shocking, but you need to know what's out there, and what the risks are of going down this path.'

The next five minutes is a blur of extremely thin and beautiful girls posing in mirrors in tiny pairs of knickers, or lying next to white cats on white sheets looking angular and emaciated and tragic. Some of the pictures are a bit weird: there's one where a girl has her thigh in both hands and her thumbs crossed over on top of it. There are a lot of ribs, and navels, and denim shorts, and crop tops. But mainly these girls just look like standard celebrities or dancers. They are not really that much thinner than the models and actresses that everyone aspires to be: the ones who play normal people in all the films and

68

adverts that everybody watches. The only difference is that their posts say things like 'I binged so much today I really hate myself rn' or 'I am so fat and stupid and I ate too much today. Tomorrow I have to restrict more' or 'I'm working out right now because I binged so much this morning'. It is obvious that 'binging' in this context means eating anything at all. Some of the comments are encouraging – 'You can do it you're so beautiful' – and some are offers of help. Anastasia expertly navigates various feeds until she finds one that features an especially beautiful girl and is all in black and white, with captions like 'I want to disappear' and 'I want smaller breasts' and 'I just looked at donuts and I got so anxious I wanted to die'. In one of the pictures the girl is wearing what looks like a child's bra-and-knickers set with the words *Daddy's Girl* embroidered on both pieces. It is actually quite creepy. The caption on the most recent picture says 'I'm going to starve until I am thin enough'. It was posted three years ago.

The question and answer session goes on for almost half an hour.

'What do you think of treacle tart?' someone asks. 'Is it really unhealthy?'

'Well, everyone's different,' begins Anastasia. 'But personally? It's still a no for me. I don't eat gluten and so that rules out most tarts. And I mean treacle does have a lot of vitamins, but the sugar content means it's still not a viable option. But that's just me – everyone has their own choices to make. Everyone has their own food boundaries, which I totally respect.'

'Do you eat dib-dobs?'

The sound of suppressed giggles.

'I honestly don't know what they are?'

'If you had to choose between being ugly and happy, or beautiful and miserable, which would you pick?'

And then the bell rings for the second period and everyone scatters.

*

Madame Vincent is directing the French nativity play that is going to be performed for the parents on the last day of term, after which the girls will be driven away for two weeks of friendless overeating and unsupervised YouTube binges. Their parents don't even know what YouTube is. They think it's all harmless pop videos and instructions for making gnocchi and putting up shelves. They have no idea that you can spend literally the whole day watching someone's butt workouts, or their abs-and-arms days. They have no idea how something like that makes you feel: both empty and full, like a dirty room with the door left open. Anastasia has uploaded approximately thirty hours' worth of footage of her eating raw food as part of her 'recovery'. These new salads, she explains in her intros, are better than her anorexic ones because they have a few macadamia nuts in them, and a teaspoon of chia seeds. You can also watch haul videos for hours and hours. Girls who order a couple of hundred quid's worth of clothes from Topshop or Pretty Little Thing and then film themselves trying on the whole lot.

But there's a lot of term still to go, somehow, before that. And the French play.

Natasha is cast as Joseph. Tiffanie is the donkey. Becky with the bad hair is Mary, well, *Marie*. Natasha's main lines involve her saying the Hail Mary in French. Something about the prayer is rhythmic, almost jazzy, with its 4/4 beat and its light swing. In the dark weeks of term Tash gets in the habit of saying it before she goes to sleep at night. She also says it during those terrible moments at 3 a.m. when she wakes with turbulence in her heart and fluorescent thoughts streaking through her brain: her father, and Bianca, and the man on the Tube, and Nico . . . She says it over and over again until it enters her dreams and she knows she is, finally, asleep. Although there is of course a difference between knowing you're asleep and actually being asleep.

Je vous salue, Marie, plein de grâce, Le Seigneur est avec vous. There's something in it about praying for poor fishermen, and it ends with the words Now, and at the hour of our death, amen. But it sounds better in French, of course: Maintenant, et à l'heure de notre mort, amen. It is beautiful. Tash has no religion, not really, and so this becomes her religion: this one prayer is all she needs. She says it, silently, on the weekly cloaked visit to the village church when everyone is invited to pray. Sometimes she also prays for peace, and joy, and to be thin. Sometimes she even prays for the villagers, that they might become thin too. She pleads with God to bless them, with their vast stomachs and fat faces. She asks that God bless them despite their ugliness and misery, and prays that He might bring light and lightness into their lives.

*

Miss Annabel is thinking about pink lilies and mauve gladioli. No one has bought her freesias for a very long time. Where do they sell freesias? Not the hideous retail park where Sin-Jin has gone for the girls' Tampax and cotton wool. Winter is approaching, and the time for such things is gone. Miss Annabel removes all the doilies from her chest of drawers. She half-heartedly dusts it and then takes out her winter perfume and puts it where the summer one has been all these months. They go fast now, the months. She finds her fingerless gloves, which she will need in the studio, even though she heats it to a point where the girls feel uncomfortable and the ones on diets get a bit fainty. Miss Annabel likes it when they faint. It proves that they do not know everything: that they should listen. She wishes that Bianca had listened. She knew what Bianca was doing when she found her posing in the mirrors in the studio, arranged so that her pointe shoes

72

were the largest thing in the image, her starveling limbs so tiny, and jointed like a puppet's. She pinches the skin on the inside of her wrist again, and it turns a pleasing iris blue before fading to the colour of pink lilies and then mauve gladioli. She does it again and again, because she knows, and she has done nothing.

*

'This is how you treat an outbreak of anorexia?' asks an angry parent, having found out about the early morning swims and the afternoon runs. 'Are you out of your fucking minds?'

So now there are new punishments. Every night after supper the girls – the bad ones, the rotting apples from the attic dorms – walk past the pictures of Princess Augusta in the lake and into the headmaster's study where he reads to them from *Great Expectations*, a story of a boy called Pip who will do anything for a beautiful, thin, rich girl called Estella, who never eats and who lives in a house full of cobwebs. No one enjoys the story that much until Estella appears in it. But a girl who delights in making a boy cry? And makes him eat, but does not ever eat herself? Everyone can get behind a character like that. Pip loves the very hem of Estella's dress. She makes him hate his hands.

Instead of calling everyone Océane, Tiffanie now calls everyone Estella.

73

'Estella, where are you go-*ange?*' she asks Rachel one afternoon. It's that darkish, gossamery time between the end of the school day and the beginning of prep. Rachel is in her sports stuff. Her thighs heave in her green regulation shorts. Surely you can get the shorts in a size bigger than the one she has got? Maybe she's just got fatter this term. Who knows?

'For a run,' says Rachel.

'But we don't have to do that any more,' says Donya.

Rachel shrugs. 'I enjoyed it,' she says. 'Thought I'd carry on.'

'It is freeze-*ange!*'

'I don't care.'

Later, after dinner, Rachel leaves her pudding for the first time ever. Prior to this she had no idea, no fucking idea, that leaving something could be even more pleasurable than eating it. Why has she never tried this before? And the feeling of giving it to Donya instead, of watching Donya masticating like a little machine, a gross cement-mixer, her flabby, spotty jaw so far away from the 2D perfection that they all want, more, even, surely, than life itself . . . ? It's beautiful, and awful, and very, very simple. Rachel takes a deep breath and begins the next chapter of her life.

*

There is a permanent haze of civet and oak moss, or

whatever they use now. No one makes perfumes with the scent glands of snakes or cats any more, but the attic dorms smell as if they do. Tash has a bullet-shaped bottle that smells a bit like home, like fictional large men from home, large men with taut muscles driving their horses over snowy hills with furs and leather.

The samples they brought back from Stevenage are almost gone. Good job, then, that they are going to Cambridge tomorrow. They are going to get more perfume samples, and stock up on cigarettes, and buy alcohol for the Christmas party: for Bianca's wake. They are all onto the headier Stevenage perfumes now: the ones they didn't like at first; the ones that smell, frankly, like sex slaves being fed to tigers.

'I can't bear Guerlain perfume,' declares Lissa, and locks herself in one of the bathrooms and showers for much longer than a normal person would. Her shower gel smells like green things and clean boys. Over the sound of the water they can hear her sobbing.

All of this is the sign of a good story to come; everyone knows that. But good stories have to be coaxed out carefully, like breech kittens; dug up slowly like hexed treasure; eased into the world gently, like an outsize poo.

'Estella,' says Tiffanie, at the bathroom door. 'ESTELLA. Don't be so stu-*peed*.'

Eventually Lissa emerges and gets into Danielle's bed. Her eyes are red. One of her arms is bleeding a little. It bleeds onto Dani's pillow, which so recently was

75

Bianca's pillow. Has the pillowcase even been changed? Perhaps not. There must still be bits of Bianca's hair and dead skin everywhere: pale fragments of a dead girl.

It was shopping with her mother, before the divorce, Lissa explains. In some small town with a spa hotel and a twee high street, perhaps somewhere in Somerset? An overheard comment in a boutique from the shop's owner, who was swathing her mother in sexclothes for him, the hedge-fund manager from Boston who is now her step-father, and who touched her leg that time deliberately and wants to sell the ponies and actually hit Suze during that awful argument, but anyway, that is not in this story.

The dark bulbs in the shop that made customers look thinner and taller, like an Instagram filter, like a cursed jewel.

'Make him remember you,' whispered the shop owner, spraying Lissa's mother with Guerlain. 'Always wear enough perfume so that he remembers you, so that when you leave the room your scent lingers for hours and hours.'

As if Lissa's mother had never worn perfume before; had never even worn clothes.

The hotel room smelled sweet and intense afterwards, dead flowers on a dark lake.

Make him remember you. Fill his office with your spray. Let him open you like a flower. That's what the woman in the shop said. While her customer's fifteen-year-old daughter was listening but pretending not to, touching the limp garments on the rails and wondering what it would be like to have to buy jeans that cost £300 rather than the ones from Topshop that her friends wear. Mom jeans. Fat, rich mom jeans. The owner of the shop draped over her counter like the remains of a dead animal, her hair thick with dry shampoo, her face caked in expensive make-up that did not conceal her triple chin and her greedy eyes.

*

It's Miss Annabel and Dr Morgan on the coach with them for the Cambridge trip. Some of the teachers have a mysterious sort of chemistry between them. For example, everyone knows that Dr Morgan hates Madame Vincent. He never meets her eye, and whenever he asks her to do something – pass him a book, hold his coffee for a second while he finds his key – he does it in that mean, annoyed voice with a sigh at the end. It's fascinating watching them. Their awkward movements are those of Guignols operated by people with stiff cold hands.

There is, disappointingly, no chemistry at all between Miss Annabel and Dr Morgan. There is, however, something going on between Becky with the bad hair and Dr Morgan. She insists on sitting next to him on the coach to 'help' count people in and count them out. This is the kind of thing a future Head Girl should be doing, but there's more to it than that. He glances at her a few times too often, then looks pale, like someone about to throw up.

The coach parks near Cambridge train station, so it's a longish walk into town. Lissa's house isn't too far away – a village about five miles out – and so she knows her way around. She comes here on the bus in the holidays. Sometimes Rachel stays with her and rides Suze's pony, and they run errands for her, for Suze: Lissa's glamorous older sister, who has no time for ponies any more. Suze has long blonde hair and her bra size is 28DD. She often gets marriage proposals in public, men going down on one knee in the middle of the street, or in the foyer of the cinema. Imagine being propositioned amidst the sour smell of cheap popcorn and factory-made butter. Imagine the crap that would stick to his knee. But everyone loves stories of Suze.

Quickly, the bad apples roll away from the heap. They tumble down a little street, past a college building. They are a bit more respectable today. Miss Annabel is stricter than Mr Hendrix. She understands about skirts. So Tiffanie is in something tweed, instead of the leather. It's pink and, now she's rolled it up a couple of times, quite short. Lissa is wearing a paper-bag skirt from Topshop that can't be rolled up, but is quite short anyway. Tash is wearing her Halpern skirt because it has not occurred to her to buy another one. Her mother, after all, owns one of everything: one skirt, one dress, one pair of trousers and one pair of Levi's jeans, once apparently so coveted. She has a fur coat, given to her by a man. Everything else is house-clothes, or the old Aeroflot cabin crew uniforms that she refuses to throw out. It's a capsule wardrobe: the capsule wardrobe of a poor woman who used to be beautiful and who still speaks fluent English and whom no one truly understands.

But that world, Natasha's ex-world, does not really exist now. It's locked away in another dimension, like Nico's aliens. There is only this world, the one with the fluorescence, the one ruled by Tash's father. But where is he? Aunt Sonja said something about him being at 'the castle' for Christmas, but Tash has no idea what that means. What castle?

The girls have brought rucksacks for the alcohol and the cigarettes. Miss Annabel has already eyed the rucksacks suspiciously but been told firmly that this is for the *environment*, because doesn't she understand that we don't *have* a Planet B? Doesn't she know how many turtles have to be killed to produce *one* plastic bag? At the mention of the turtles Dr Morgan started freezing them with his biologist's death-stare, but then Becky with the bad hair asked him to help her reach *her* rucksack down from the overhead compartment and inadvertently normalised the carrying of rucksacks. Why has she brought one? No one cares.

The apples roll into John Lewis and ask for perfume samples, but they are not so impressive in this big university town. The over-highlighted, blusher-crazed ladies

79

here aren't as intimidated by their cheekbones as the ones in Stevenage were. To get people properly impressed with their cheekbones the girls will need to find men: desperate men without wives or scruples. Suze likes drinking in a pub called the Marionette ('drinking in' not 'going to'), where many people have proposed to her of a late Friday night. Lissa puts into Maps this fabled place she has heard so much about, and the bad apples roll on and on doing what Siri tells them until they come to rest in a dingy back street that smells of death and putrefaction. No one said the pub would be this rundown. Can they go in? No one wants to, so Tash goes first. It can't be worse than communism. Or what they say communism was.

The door is wooden and closed. Tash twists the handle and pushes it open, just slightly. There's a fug inside, fingering its way towards them. The threshold smells of men: their heft and their erections and their cruel laughter because you stood in the wrong place and you asked for the wrong thing and you are a child and so guess what no erection for you in fact and no vodka and orange either because that is a child's drink and you should have known that and where are your parents . . . ?

Where *are* her parents?

The bad apples roll backwards and then in the direction of a tea shop for old people, with dusty cakes and greyish doilies. At least here they know the rules. Here are aged hens like Sin-Jin and Miss Annabel clucking over pictures of their grandchildren (not that Sin-Jin or Miss Annabel have such things because of the tragic and wasted lives they have spent at the school). Here are vast sandwich cakes with jam the colour of heavy periods, and hard, chewy croissants, and meringues that look like Tiffanie's tits except for being pinker.

Lissa texts Suze. *We're in Cambridge. Can you buy us alcohol for our end of term party?* Suze texts back: *Fuck off.* Lissa tries again: *Please please please oh beautiful sister?* Suze eventually replies with the name of a small old-fashioned off-licence with an owner called Bob. *He likes young girls,* she says. *But don't say I told you that. Just smile and let him see slightly down your top and he won't ask for ID. If you tell Mum I'll fucking kill you.*

*

The Malibu tastes like medicine. Tash thought it would taste nice. It's supposed to taste of coconuts and desert islands and holidays, not that Tash has ever had a foreign holiday. She'd never even flown before coming here.

She and Tiffanie are locked in an attic bathroom with one bottle of Malibu: Lissa, Rachel and Danielle are locked in a different bathroom with the other, although it's a fair guess that Rachel isn't drinking much now she's so healthy. Donya isn't allowed to drink because of her religion, so she's acting as lookout. Why doesn't Malibu taste nice? It's as disappointing as smoking the first time,

81

and coffee. Do you get to an age where liking these things is automatic, or do you have to learn it? It's cold on the bathroom floor, where Tash is sitting. Tiffanie is sprawled in the bath, one leg hanging out, with her silk dressing gown open over a black bandage dress.

'Dis-goose-*tange*,' says Tiffanie.

'Yeah,' says Tash. 'Oui. Je sais. Mais . . .' She shrugs and takes another swig.

'Where are you go-*ange* for ex-mass?' asks Tiffanie.

'Aunt Sonja,' says Tash. 'London. Then some castle. I don't know.'

'And your mother?'

Tash shrugs. Passes the bottle to Tiffanie, whose hand dangles over the edge of the bath. Her fingernails are a strange Oriental shade of green that's almost blue.

'It's cold in Russia. Better to stay here. You?'

'Paris, bien sûr,' says Tiffanie. For Tiffanie, only two places ever exist: wherever she is at that moment, and Paris.

'Why are you at school in England?' asks Tash.

'C'est cheap.' She shrugs. 'Thérèse est ici. My father is the cousin of her father, so. They are rich together in bonking.'

Bonking? Right: *banking*. Tash takes the Malibu back and swigs.

'If they're rich, then . . . ?'

'Rich people love the économique, of course. Why are you here?' Tiffanie asks.

'I didn't know my father until last year. He found me. He's rich.'

'Mais not that rich,' says Tiffanie. 'Because it is so cheap to come here.'

'Perhaps. I don't know. I think he might have a helicopter?'

'Quoi?'

Tash mimes flying. When Tiffanie says 'le avion', she shakes her head and twists her finger round and round.

'Ah! Hélicoptère,' says Tiffanie.

Tash laughs. 'That's what I said, *Estella.*'

'Je suis pas Estella. Je suis Aunt Sonja,' says Tiffanie, with a wink.

'Et moi?'

'You are Princess Aw-goose-ta,' says Tiffanie. A pause. 'Avec les GHDs.'

Princess Augusta with hair straighteners. 'Yeah, maybe. Bianca probably looked more like Princess Augusta.'

'Oui.' She sighs. 'Bianca.'

Tash sighs too. 'Yeah.'

'Quand même, ceci est un privet school pour les économiques. Les pauvres.'

Les pauvres pêcheurs. The poor fishermen. Tash laughs.

'Les fishermen,' she says. 'Les men du fish. This is a school for fishermen?'

Tiffanie laughs too, with her head back on the white porcelain of the old bath. She opens her green eyes wide and in them Tash sees perfect simplicity, perfect friendship.

They could just as easily be toddlers in a nursery, or kittens in a basket. She goes to swig from the bottle and realises there isn't much left, so she passes it back. She doesn't feel that different yet, except she wants to undress and get Tiffanie to replay the tutorial she gave them all last week on the uses of tit-tape and she wants to write to Nico and tell him she does in fact like his tongue and . . . Tash blinks.

'Not fishmen,' says Tiffanie. 'The poor rich. *Les pauvres riches*.'

'Is that a thing?'

'Mais oui.'

'Do you feel drunk?'

'Oui.'

'Shall we go to the disco?'

'Oui, Estella!'

It's more difficult than they thought, getting up. They giggle and sit back down. Perhaps they'll try again in ten minutes, or never. Maybe they'll have to stay here forever. They are windlestraws. Mere fluff. This is ridiculously funny, and—

Someone's knocking at the door. A teacher? Big eyes. Silence.

'Tiffanie? Tash?' It's Donya's voice.

'Oui?' A giggle. 'Do you have a dib-dob?'

'No! Shhh. You have to come out. They're asking about you downstairs. Becky's going to tell the teachers that you're drinking.'

'Merde,' says Tiffanie.

Tash gets up. She feels amazing and awful at the same time. She could fly, really fly, with her own little cobwebby wings. She could soar through the air, if only she didn't feel so . . . so . . .

'I think I'm going to be—'

'Estella!'

*

Dr Morgan struggles to like the girls' choice of music, with its vocoders and sudden, vertiginous changes in BPM. Each song is like three songs rolled into one. Three bad songs. Everything this generation likes is corrupt or degraded in some way: tinny music on cheap head-phones; tragically low-res MP3s. He looks at Madame Vincent when he doesn't think she will notice. She is the same vintage as the LPs he covets but never buys. She is as solid and unbreakable as vinyl. She is analogue, old-school. Her natural-tan tights are wrinkled behind her knees in thin folds that do not conceal her varicose veins. He thinks of the hot nothingness she makes him feel, like whisky hitting your throat. But not now: he doesn't feel that *now*. He only feels it in the dark times, when he has given in and stopped struggling and gone under.

His lungs filling with algae. His absolute need for that pain.

Her flesh that is slightly powdery and smells of stale roses.

He sometimes sees his problem as a beaker that will not fill. At the bottom of the beaker are the girls and their classes and meals and registration and the crushlets swarming like little clouds of insects and the older girls starting to look at him and then look away. Except . . . But we're not there yet. The next part of the beaker is his work: meaningless, of course. You don't change the world as a biology teacher in a school like this full of ridiculous little madams with their contraband lipstick and their all-consuming eating disorders and their lack of profound thought. *Stimulating young minds.* That's what the job advert had said. These minds do not need further stimulation, of that he is sure. Quite what they need he doesn't know. His days are filled with waiting for them to end. He reads *New Scientist.* Does crosswords. Sends letters to newspapers. Sends off the crosswords.

That is a life. That is enough. It is.

He no longer prays, but he does read every email sent by the Humanist Society.

So why will the beaker not fill? It's not that it doesn't want to: it wants to fill and froth and steam and spill over like those ridiculous pictures of drinks on social media that the older girls like. The effervescence of online role-playing games. The things he sometimes accidentally sees on his iPhone's Private Browsing mode, when his fingers type words into search engines that come from a part of his mind he cannot completely control. Not the whole phrase, just part of it. *Boys. Spanking by. Female teacher.* If your fingers add the word *hentai* you get Japanese cartoons instead of real people, which are better because a) they are cleaner, and b) you can feel less guilty. The only problem is that the Japanese *really* like pictures of well-endowed male teachers giving it to their young – like paedophilically young and extremely tiny – female students, which is such a dumb thing to be looking at in a girls' school even on Private Browsing mode. And anyway, these images are not the ones he wants. He wants women to be towering, high-heeled, armed with riding crops and mean. Like Madame Vincent is some-times, when she is in the right mood. The froth pulses like liquid nitrogen, fizzes like those stupid experiments with magnesium that he does for the crushlets, but does not spill. Not yet.

Becky from Year 11.

Not in reality, of course, but in his mind. In the froth. Lost in it.

All the things in the froth are wrong. They bubble over and never settle. OK, they stop him thinking about the rest of the beaker for a few hours but then if he's not careful he is up all night doing beastly things, the things the village boys no doubt also do, perhaps more often but not with such vile intensity, such desperate concen-tration, such animal depth.

'Sir?'

'What is it now, Becky?'

'My name's Donya, sir.'

'What is it, Donya?

'Can you help us, sir? It's Tash and Tiffanie. They're a little bit ill.'

*

'Always make sure you have two paths,' says Aunt Sonja.

They are in Selfridges, having tea. Natasha is avoiding anything that tastes like coconut. At the back of her gullet there is still the thick pukey whiteness of the Malibu. The gluey sweetness of it. Like tropical sperm, not that anyone would say that at school. It's more the kind of thing they would say at home, the kids on the street and their brown-toothed mothers with their polyester cold-shoulder tops. They probably vomit all the time from alcohol. Natasha is never drinking again. She does not want to be those women; she barely wants to be herself. She wants to be pure inside like she used to be. Pure and slight like a backslash.

It is warm for Christmas week. The Christmas floor in Selfridges has been ready for all this since August, which is when all the mentally ill people bought their baubles. Is excess of sentimentality a mental illness? It should be. A lack of it is. That's what Estella had; what was wrong with her. She was beautiful but had no heart. That's what she says to Pip. If you could choose one

88

or the other, what would it be? An excess of sentimentality or its absence? But really, though? Or is that a two-paths situation? What exactly does Aunt Sonja mean?

'Two paths?' says Tash.

'Two *potential* paths. Choice. The chance to go in a different direction. Don't go so far down a path that you can't go back. Never go through a door that closes behind you. Leave the door open. That is the most important thing. I don't mean in real life, although that is not a bad idea too. It's a metaphor: an image. Do not do anything that's undoable.'

Tash looks at her hands. The backs of her wrists. Her forearms.

'You mean like a tattoo?'

Aunt Sonja shakes her head. 'Get all the tattoos you want,' she says. 'Especially if you don't want to get married.'

Tash is not sure exactly what that means. Aunt Sonja is expressionless.

'No,' Aunt Sonja says. 'I mean conceptually.' She taps her head. 'In here. You smoke, right?'

'No.' One breath. Two. 'OK, yes. Sometimes.'

'Have you passed the point where you choose to smoke? Do you *have* to do it now?'

Natasha feels the stirring of a little creature inside her. A worm that needs feeding. A worm that was born back in Russia, by the old bomb crater behind her school. A

89

group of them smoking for the first time, while Nico's sister stood there smiling and coaxing.

'Yes, I think so.'

'That's a mistake,' says Aunt Sonja. 'But you can use it to learn. Don't let anything else give you that feeling. Some people are addicted to eating, for example. They eat as much as they can, and they are compelled to do it even when they don't want to. Look over there.' She gestures with her head to a girl of about Natasha's age sitting on her own at one of the tables. She has a black headscarf and a chubby face. Tash has already noticed her. She's basically bingeing in public. She has a whole afternoon tea to herself: three tiers of cakes and sandwiches. She's eating her way through it as if this is an unpleasant task she has to complete as soon as possible so she can tick it off. But she also looks kind of like she will never complete the task, like that philosophy guy who has to keep rolling the rock uphill. Although rolling a rock uphill at least burns calories.

'She doesn't look very happy,' Tash says.

'Maybe she is. Who knows? Who are we to judge?'

'Um . . .'

'Maybe she hasn't eaten for days. Maybe she's celebrating. But I don't think so. I agree with you. She looks miserable. She's taken a path to a place that it is hard to come back from. She's not choosing to do this any more. She can't stop. It's the same with alcohol. Cocaine. Masturbation, for some people. Dildos. Some people can't help themselves visiting prostitutes. They say this will be the last time, but it is never the last time.'

Tash feels awkward. 'Maybe we should stop staring?'

'Yes. True. We don't want to make her feel worse.' Aunt Sonja looks at Tash. 'Don't let the door close behind you,' she says. She sips her Darjeeling tea. 'Even – especially – if you feel like you have entered paradise. I've had a letter from the school. You're all anorexic, apparently. Is that true?'

'No.'

'But there has been some death?'

'One girl died. She was my friend. But . . .'

'But what?'

'I don't think it was that. I don't think it was anorexia.'

'Why?'

'I don't know. I mean, she drowned in a lake.'

'OK . . .'

'I mean, she didn't starve.'

'Drowned?' Aunt Sonja is nodding. 'Or was simply *found* there?'

'I don't know.'

'Are people talking about this? Are they making theories?'

'No.'

'But you are making a theory?'

'I don't know.'

*

Christmas Eve dinner is brown rice and baked fish with broccoli. There is homemade chocolate mousse for pudding. The mousse has two ingredients: eggs and bitter chocolate. It has been setting in the fridge since first thing this morning when Aunt Sonja separated the eggs and melted the chocolate while listening to an English choir on Radio 3.

On Christmas morning, Aunt Sonja gives Natasha a paperback copy of the book *Londongrad*, about Russian oligarchs who come to London. 'It's all true,' she says. Aunt Sonja also gives Tash a black Balmain dress with gold buttons in a French size 36, a pair of strappy Versace sandals, a Chanel lipstick in the shade Monte Carlo and a small pair of diamond earrings. Last of all, she gives her a Net-a-Porter gift box. 'From your father,' says Aunt Sonja. Inside is a large white-gold and black-diamond bracelet from De Grisogono that looks like a fan or a snake's head. Tash is not sure she likes it, but she puts it on anyway. Then Aunt Sonja tells Tash to pack an overnight bag with these things and a toothbrush and whatever toiletries you need if you are a beautiful, clear-skinned fifteen-year-old. Some underwear; probably not a bra but ideally you need a thong with this dress. Tit-tape? Perhaps.

They go out for Christmas lunch to a private members' club in Soho. Tash wonders what Aunt Sonja would be doing if she were not here. Most other people are in cheerful groups; they have the only table for two. She wonders where her father is; if her mother misses her. Her mother will be with Nana in the countryside by now, smoking outside by the woodshed, tapping things into her phone with her long clicky nails. She doesn't email or call Tash any more. She waits for Tash to make contact, and then she responds in a strange false voice that Tash imagines is what her mother thinks her Anglicised daughter would now want to hear, or perhaps even the opposite. It's so confusing. *Are you English yet?* her mother says. *Are you rich? Has your father given you any actual cash or just promises?* Tash doesn't know what to say. It wasn't her idea to come here. Her father sent money and her mother arranged it all through a lawyer in London called Mr Ross.

'How are your theories progressing?' asks Aunt Sonja. She is drinking a Snowball.

Natasha sighs. 'If I tell you something, please don't be angry.'

Aunt Sonja shrugs. Sips her Snowball. Switches to Russian.

'It depends what it is.'

Tash fiddles with her bracelet. 'I saw some pictures of the dead girl on Instagram.'

Aunt Sonja raises a microbladed eyebrow. 'What, not actually . . . ?'

'Oh no. Nonono, I mean she was alive in the pictures. But they all had these hashtags like "thinspo" and "starving" and stuff like that.' It had been an accident.

Tash had done it the night after Anastasia's talk. Just to see; just to have a proper look at more of those tiny pretty troubled girls and think about them. To think about their ribs and whether Tash also wanted ribs like that and what to do about it. It took longer than she expected and just at the point where she felt like she'd seen every anorexic girl on the planet, and read all their disturbing lists of #goals, she'd scrolled down, deep down into one of the weirder hashtags, and there she was: Bianca.

'These are bad feeds,' says Aunt Sonja. 'Go on.'

'OK, well, most of hers was basically just selfies. She did a lot of them in the dance studio at school, which has loads of mirrors. But . . .'

'Yes?'

'OK, some of the pictures were obviously taken by someone else.'

'A friend?'

'She didn't have any friends, apart from in her dorm, and in mine.'

'And it was not one of these friends?'

Tash shakes her head. 'No.'

'Why not?

'Just because . . . I don't know. She was so secretive about her eating disorder. She never even took her clothes off in front of us. And also, some of the pictures were of photographs. No one has photographs. They were slightly curled at the edges, like real life. Like Polaroids.

And some were in frames, but real ones, not digital.' One of Natasha's mother's English boyfriends had once had a Polaroid camera. Lyudmila would dress in her bikini and her fur coat and hold in her stomach and pose in the kitchen or on the balcony with factory smoke ruining her hair.

'And the captions? What did they say?'

'Really sad stuff,' says Tash. Should she share any of it? She suddenly realises that of course the posts are public anyway. How odd that people might find them and not realise that the girl they are looking at is dead: the girl in the white bikini posing by the double bed with crumpled white sheets and a horse sculpture and lake in the background. 'They said things like "I want to float away". Some stuff about Ophelia from *Hamlet*. Something about a black diamond.'

'Do you know *Hamlet*?'

'Not really,' says Tash. 'They did it as a ballet or something at school last year? I think Bianca was Ophelia. She was obsessed with her anyway, and Princess Augusta, of course.'

Aunt Sonja is nodding. Her eyes are closed. If it wasn't for the Botox she'd be frowning right now. She breathes slowly and then opens her eyes.

'This is becoming a very interesting case,' she says.

'*Case*?' says Natasha, but then Aunt Sonja gets a text on her phone and has to pop outside for a moment. While she is gone, Tash puts extra butter on her potatoes and mashes it in and eats it quickly, before anyone notices. That would be like an extra 5 points on Weight Watchers, but it doesn't count on Christmas Day, right? Tash tries to care and feel guilty and be the kind of person who complains to their skinny friends on Instagram that they have just binged and want to die, but she finds she actually doesn't give a shit.

On Boxing Day a car takes Natasha and Aunt Sonja to Battersea Heliport, where a helicopter is waiting for them. Taking off feels like being pulled up by a feeble thread and then dangling from it, like a spider that has been taken from the bath and is being put outside.

'We can go wherever we want!' declares Aunt Sonja over the roar of the engine. 'Because we are rich!' Or something like that. She could actually be saying anything, because it's too loud to hear. She doesn't often smile, but she smiles now, now she's in danger, and high, literally high over the sparkle of London, the eternal fluorescence.

*

Rachel contemplates the plate of food in front of her. It could be worse. She can eat the sprouts and the bit of turkey without skin. If she was taking veganism seriously she would leave the turkey as well, but she has to eat something. She knows that. She knows the dangers of 'starvation mode', where your desperate body puts on weight even with no food, and becomes able to pull grams of fat from anywhere: even body creams, even things you touch, even from the fat of people around you. That's what Tiffanie once said. She said it in a biology lesson and Dr Morgan, who was normally so mild, actually completely lost it and sent her out of the room. He looked as if he might cry afterwards, like he was the kind of person – like Rachel, like Rachel's mother – who can't get angry without also crying.

Rachel can't have the potatoes or the parsnips because they have too many grams of carbohydrate. The bread sauce is made of, well, bread. No one, literally no one, eats bread. White flour is made of all the unhealthiest bits of wheat, which has in any case been genetically modified to be addictive, like opium. That's what Rachel's older brother Elliot has told her. Refined flours get caught in the little thingummies in your gut and irritate them and then your gut gets so inflamed it rips apart and bits of white flour go zooming around in your actual blood and can even make you die or catch schizophrenia. The white sauce is made from dairy, which means the bloody pus of enslaved cows who are forcefully impregnated and have their babies taken away. Dairy gives you spots and makes you fat because it isn't designed to be eaten by adult humans. It gives you mucus, thick ropes of it coming out of your nose and sometimes going into your brain. You can drown in your own mucus, and it will serve you right.

Cranberry sauce, meanwhile, is almost entirely sugar.

Rachel saw her mother making it, first thing this morning while it was still dark outside. She was wearing her white dressing gown, the neck smeared and dark with make-up, and she was stirring an entire cup of white – WHITE – sugar into the saucepan with the frozen cranberries.

'Don't tell your brother,' she'd said to Rachel.

So many things are made entirely from sugar. Bread, quite apart from everything else, turns into a bowl of sugar in your stomach. Literally a whole bowl. The same is true of fruit. Fruit nowadays has been specifically bred by insatiable, corrupt farmers to be full of sugar. Unless you pick your own fruit in the wild, you may as well be eating a bag of Haribo (which are nicer; let's be honest). Roast potatoes are also sugar, but coated in fat and burnt so they give you cancer. Rachel's mum does them in goose fat, which is so gross it doesn't bear thinking about. The parsnips are the same, but just taste worse than the potatoes.

The fat girl Rachel used to be, the one who had seconds and thirds of roast potatoes, and roast-potato sandwiches on Boxing Day, and a whole tin of Roses to herself, is gone. She is dead. Buried. Decomposed. Now she shares her brother's bowl of quinoa that he's insisted on having because it is healthy and all this other crap is not. He's a vegan, but he says Rachel shouldn't become one quite yet. She should follow a paleo diet until she is thin and then she should transition to being plant-based. He's barely spoken to her for the last few years, and now all this.

The gym opens on Boxing Day and Elliot takes Rachel with him and this time doesn't make her hide in the cardio section and pretend not to be his sister while he hangs out with his mates in the weights room. Her old gym stuff already doesn't fit her, so this morning Rachel snuck into her mother's bedroom and found a pair of Sweaty Betty leggings and a black Nike top which she put over a pink sports bra that used to be too small for her but isn't now. She's layered up some necklaces and wears an ear-cuff that looks almost like a helix piercing. When she loses another stone she's going to get her navel done. She's chosen the silver dreamcatcher crystal belly bar she wants from Claire's Accessories. She looks at it every day. For the first time ever, she knows that something like that could be hers. So far, this is the best Christmas ever.

OK, so no one knows exactly where her father is after all the shouting at the end of Christmas Day, and her grandmother has maybe a week or two left to live, and her sister is back in rehab and— Who cares about all that? Jordon looks at her today: he actually does. He refers to her at one point – in all seriousness – as Elliot's 'hot little sister'. And everyone compliments her and gives her advice and even the terrifying fitness instructor twins, Millie and Izzy, look admiringly at Rachel's arms and midsection and ask her things about her diet and her running programme and for the first time in her life Rachel falls asleep feeling warm and happy and free.

After all these years she has the answer. SHE HAS THE ANSWER. It was right in front of her all along, like a handsome prince in disguise, a darkling frog.

*

The castle is on an island you can only reach by air. It is in Scotland. Or maybe Ireland. Some Celtic cold place. They land on the helipad and crunch down a gravel path where they are greeted by someone. A butler? Tash doesn't know what you would call this person, but he is obviously staff. He has a clipboard and shiny shoes. He shakes hands with Aunt Sonja.

'The young people are in the hot tubs,' he says to Natasha. He takes her bag. 'I'll show you your room, where you can get ready.'

Natasha follows him in through a side door. It's like school. She follows him up back-stairways, along carpets that have seen better days, down a corridor cold from an open window, the smell of mildew in the air. Then a longer, wider corridor with large white spaces on the walls where paintings used to be, and wires poking out of light fittings.

Tash thinks of the paintings in the headmaster's study. All those horses.

'Not long moved in,' says the butler. 'Chaos, really.'

She has not brought a bikini. Really, she should stay in her room and get ready for this evening. She should not be distracted with young people and hot tubs. Is her father going to be here? A thrill runs through her. She's almost forgotten what he looks like. When she tries to make a picture of him in her head, all that comes is an ageing pop star. What's his name? Paul McCartney. Father of Stella, who makes the sports clothes. Then comes the image of Tiffanie writing to him, the ancient Beatle Sir Paul, with her turquoise French fountain pen, asking if he is really dead, because of the rumours about the *Abbey Road* album cover. The girls adore *Abbey Road*. They found the CD under Bianca's bed, along with some sheet music and three carrier bags containing mouldering, half-chewed food. Surely, Natasha thought then, surely if someone was going to commit suicide they would not leave secret carrier bags of food under their bed? Surely Bianca wouldn't want people to see that? But Tash didn't know why she thought that or if it was even true. She didn't say anything to the others. She just joined in when everyone said how gross it was and then quietly disposed of the bags in the large bins outside the kitchens.

She tries again to think of her father. Nope. Nico? Nope. Her mother? Yes, she can still see her mother: the hair extensions and the fake breasts and the kitchen table covered with application forms and a massive ashtray.

The hot tubs. Tash walks over to the window and looks out onto large gardens, then cliffs, then sea. She fancies she hears splashing and whooping. What even is a hot tub in this country, in the winter? *The young people.* Why is that so compelling? She should stay here and do her hair and make-up the way Tiffanie showed her, but she wants to find the young people. She wants to know how to be one of them. So it's back down the corridors, that same lost feeling she still has at school. A side door.

It's not splashing she hears first, but the clinking of glasses.

The hot tubs are across the gardens, beyond a maze she is glad she didn't try to walk through. It's freezing. Not as cold as home, of course, but how would you get to the hot tubs in a bikini even if you had one? What would you wear on your feet?

Two large brass capsules looking out over the sea. Steam rising from them like a twinkless winter mist. There is a waiter standing to one side by a table with ice buckets with champagne in them. His face is expressionless. Is this serious?

'Who the fuck are you?' comes a deep, confident voice from one of the hot tubs.

He would be attractive if it wasn't for the sneer. Dark hair; pale skin. He looks Tash up and down as if she is something he has ordered online. In the tub with him is another teenage boy with red hair and massive freckles. They are both around sixteen, maybe seventeen. In the other tub are four thin, blonde girls. They also look Tash up and down, and she suddenly sees what they are seeing. The slight curve in her cheeks. The DD breasts that have come from nowhere this year. The moon-like shape of her bum.

Tash's legs suddenly feel like they are made out of the stuff in Bianca's carrier bags.

'Who the fuck are *you*?' she says back before she can stop herself. She wants to sound badass, but all she can hear is the Russian accent that they are all hearing. The broken reed of her voice. Her words sounding childish; not clever, not flirtatious.

'He's Teddy Ross,' says the freckled friend. 'And you must be Natasha, the mail-order Russian bride.'

The girls in the other hot tub laugh, their bodies bobbing up and down like hard pieces of fusilli coming to the boil.

'Really?' says Tash. 'I don't think so.'

Her legs. The rancid food wobbling, unable to hold her up. Her breath, frozen somewhere between her chest and her mouth. Her ridiculous heartbeat. Her glimmerless life. She turns, shakily, and leaves, like an am-dram nobody who has fucked up the only line she ever had.

When Tash gets back to her room she feels cold and stupid. She puts on the Balmain dress with no pleasure and realises she looks fat in it, even in the 36. She is huge. She protrudes. She is a protuberance. A massive bulge. A cartoon of a stick woman covered in semi-circles. If she allows herself to breathe out she actually looks pregnant. She is simply enormous. The largest woman in the castle, certainly, but perhaps even on the planet.

103

The dinner is in a large dining room with a lot of different-sized glasses and white napkins. Natasha is seated between two old English ladies who have a conversation over her about problems to do with interior designers, first-class rail travel, the editor of the *Telegraph* and a dangerous communist called Jeremy Corbyn. Natasha has trouble with the food. There is too much of it. It is not vegetarian. She does not know how to eat it. Some of it is slimy.

'Are you one of the prostitutes, dear?' the lady on her left asks her, during pudding.

At least that's what Tash thinks she says, as brown juice from the crème caramel drips down her tired, powdered face.

*

Back at school there's no quinoa. Rachel looks at the lunch Mrs Cuckoo has made and there is nothing, literally nothing, to eat. She takes a plateful of green beans and some pineapple and feels so happy when a few of the other girls do the same. Are they actually copying her because they want what she now has? Everyone is fascinated with her. They examine her body in excruciating detail, and she loves it. She really loves it. Tiffanie, who usually ignores Rachel completely, actually feels her biceps and smiles and winks.

It's now that sad sleepy time on a Sunday evening.

Everyone has changed out of their travel skirts and into jeans or leggings. Rachel has gone for a run, which isn't really allowed in the dark, but with all the bright lights in the school no one can really see what's going on outside. No one can see the hibernating animals, or the dead spiders and their rotten webs. The tenebrous lake.

After supper Sin-Jin appears in the Year 11 common room.

'Girls,' she says to the apples, who are in the corner hogging the CD player as usual, playing their out-dated music on out-dated tech. She raises her eyebrows and they know what this means. They've been sort of waiting for this.

They follow her to the headmaster's office. So word has finally got out about the party, then. The Malibu. All the endless pale puke and Tash and Tiffanie lying there like Snow White. That was what Lissa said to Tash, that she looked like Snow White. Could Tash be thought of like that, as actually beautiful? She's never really thought of it before. Anyway, stupid Dr Morgan said he wouldn't tell, but of course he did. He's an adult and a teacher and they are not Becky with the bad hair so—

'Thank you for coming, girls,' says Dr Moone in his grave voice. He's sitting behind his vast desk and they are all standing haphazardly in front of it like they have been gathered together in a bucket: apples ready to be bobbed by children with sharp teeth, or kittens ready to be given away to whoever will have them, or else . . . He takes a

105

deep breath. 'I'm afraid there's been another incident. Some of you undoubtedly know about it already. I'm going to have to ask once again for your complete confidentiality on this.'

'Of course, sir,' murmurs Rachel.

'Yes,' says Lissa. 'Absolutely.'

Tash glances at Tiffanie. Donya and Dani look at the ground.

'I understand that all of you were involved with the incident at the Christmas party,' says Dr Moone. 'Now, although you should be in trouble for bringing alcohol into the school, we will put that to one side for the moment, because it seems that two of you went through a rather regrettable ordeal.' He looks at his desk. 'Which, I'm afraid, has only come to light over the break.'

Glances and side-eyes and half-frowns.

'We are going to need to talk separately to the two girls who were drinking.'

Tash breathes in. Her legs feel strange and weightless. She looks at Tiffanie. Of course, they were all supposed to be drinking except Donya, but the others didn't like the Malibu and went downstairs for Diet Coke instead. They pretended to be drunk but were not drunk. Everyone sort of vaguely knows this without really knowing it, but in any case the headline events of the evening involved Tash and Tiffanie vomiting so much they literally almost died, and Dr Morgan secretly helping them to bed and everyone promising never to tell.

'We are going to organise counselling for all of you,' says Dr Moone.

Counselling? But—

'Dr Morgan is dead,' says Dr Moone. 'I'm sorry if this is a shock. I want you to know that this is not your fault.'

Tash glances at Tiffanie again. Not their fault? What's that supposed to mean?

'Once again,' says Dr Moone, 'I need to ask for your complete co-operation on this. I need you all to keep this totally confidential. The school will be responding formally to the police inquiry. If any of you are approached by the press, or by the police, you are to say nothing and come straight to me, do you understand? The tabloids love murky stories about private schools and they'll have us shut down in an instant if we handle this badly.'

'How did he die?' asks Donya.

'He drowned himself,' says Dr Moone. 'Like Bianca. Now, I need to have a few moments alone with the girls who were drinking that night, please.'

Tash and Tiffanie look at one another again. The others shuffle out of the office, glancing back and making concerned faces. Sin-Jin closes the door.

The headmaster sighs.

'We found some unpleasant pictures in with Dr Morgan's things. Don't worry: they have been destroyed. Well, all except the ones he took of Bianca Downlowe.

We will be passing those to the police. We saw no reason why the pictures he took of you girls need be part of this investigation. He is dead; Bianca is dead. The whole thing has been extremely unfortunate, but the time has come to draw a line under—'

'Pictures of *us*?' says Tash. 'I don't understand.'

'From during the *incident*,' hisses Sin-Jin.

'What incident?'

Dr Moone sighs. 'Of course, you were very drunk, and perhaps you don't remember. This is something to explore with the counsellors. We understand that Dr Morgan wasn't in the dormitory on his own with you for very long: perhaps only ten minutes. It wasn't . . .' Dr Moone's blank eyes fall and hit the desk but do not bounce. He looks up again slowly. 'It wasn't long enough for, well, the worst. We don't think the worst happened.'

This is so wrong but Tash now really, really wants to laugh. Are they saying that Dr Morgan sexually abused them in some way? That's ridiculous. When he was putting them to bed? But they had their clothes on, didn't they? And they were so drunk and probably smelled of vomit and he was actually very kind to them and, it seems, never did tell anyone. Poor, dear, sweet Dr Morgan with his terrible biology lessons and sour breath.

'When did he die?' asks Tiffanie.

'After he was confronted with the photographs. I told him I was about to alert the police and, well, I suppose he felt his life was over.'

It feels cold in the room all of a sudden. Tash thinks of how she lay in bed that night – Snow White, maybe, but with that tropical, sickly edge – still in the clothes she'd put on for the disco. Donya . . . Wasn't it *Donya* who helped them off with their clothes much later? Or Lissa. Maybe both of them. The room spinning. Getting up to be sick again. No sign of Dr Morgan then, after lights-out. Tash remembers the feeling on the Underground when that man touched her: it was confusing, and over so quickly. Could Dr Morgan have done something like that to her, but worse? She tries to feel it. She can't feel it. She tries again.

An abuse victim. A survivor of abuse. Her abuser dead in the lake.

People do forget this kind of thing, don't they? Don't they?

But of course they are changed and broken forever.

*

Another parent has written to complain about the programme of talks on eating disorders. *You are fucking crazy*, the email says. *You are really out of your pathetic fucking minds. If the girls were smoking weed, would you bring in a drug dealer to let them try heroin to see how bad it is? No, you fucking wouldn't. Well, actually, you probably would, because you have no fucking idea what you are doing and you are completely, hopelessly out of touch. Is anyone there under the age of 70? I mean, seriously, what planet do you actually think you're fucking living on? I am withdrawing my daughter as of Monday.*

And that's the end of Flick.

*

Dominic and Tony are back.

'Right,' Dominic says to Tash. 'We're going to have no fucking around here, OK? No silly laughing or messing about like last time. Getting over PTSD is no fucking picnic, I can tell you. You're going to have to co-operate with me.'

They are in a quiet room in the Dower House. Outside, Tash can see Detective Inspector Amaryllis Archer striding around the grounds in her usual jeans and high-heeled boots. Whenever she appears, Tash can't take her eyes off her. She has the same confident air that Aunt Sonja has, but without the secrecy and sadness. She is also about three stone heavier. She's not fat, not really. She's solid, a bit curvy. Should she have tucked her top into her jeans the way she has? Her boots are pointy. She wears a lot of make-up but in a sort of bold, fun way. Electric blue eyeshadow and blusher the colour of a perfect pink spring morning. She is wearing a leopard-print belt and a purple faux-fur hooded jacket and massive gold hoop earrings. She has dark skin and big hair: *really* big hair.

Tash thinks back to one of those early days in the

dorm, when Tiffanie was explaining how you come up with your personal style for each season. The secret is pairing two words that don't usually go together. Ideally, one of the words should reference a current fashion trend from this actual season and one should be something seemingly random that you have in fact spent hours and hours thinking about. So, for example, you could have cocktail safari, or mermaid outlaw, or vagabond princess, or cowgirl strip-club, or revolutionary vaudeville, or ballet tramp (which is Tiffanie's all-time favourite and involves going everywhere in beat-up ballerinas and 501s with her feet slightly turned out like Charlie Chaplin's while simultaneously channelling Harpo Marx and Anna Pavlova).

Tiffanie is in the next room with Tony.

To get over PTSD you have to really face what happened to you. You have to write it down and then read it out over and over again until it no longer bothers you. It's like people who are afraid of spiders having to sit in a room with a spider in a tank and then out of the tank and then near them and then on their actual hands. The problem is that Tash has no idea what actually happened or even if anything did. How can you let something out of its tank to crawl on you if it was never there in the first place?

She stares out of the window. You can almost see the lake from here. Amaryllis Archer's look is kind of party pirate. Tash wonders if she chose that theme deliberately at the start of this season. Tiffanie says that sometimes it's acceptable to keep a look for several seasons, like Kate Moss did in the olden days when she wore her boho roadie ensembles for literally years. Would someone like Detective Inspector Archer even have time to construct a themed look? She must be so busy solving crimes after all. Maybe it's accidental.

'. . . do you?' says Dominic.

'Sorry?' says Tash.

He breathes in for about a million years and then sighs heavily.

'You are going to have to get with the fucking programme, girlie,' he says.

'Sorry,' says Tash. She shrugs. 'But I've already said that I don't think anything actually happened with Dr Morgan.'

'But he had pictures,' says Dominic. 'Dirty pictures. Of you. And your hot French friend.'

'I haven't seen any pictures.'

'Well, they're not exactly going to show them to you, are they?'

'Why not? Especially if I'm supposed to face what's happened. I can't even remember it. Have you seen them?'

'Do I look like some kind of raging paedophile?'

'Well, I thought—'

Dominic rolls his eyes. 'Right. I'll see what I can do,' he says. 'I'll say we're not making any progress. Are you sure you want to see the pictures if I can get them?'

Tash nods. 'I'm just really not sure there are any. The headmaster said he destroyed them, but—'

'If there aren't any pictures, then why am I even fucking here?'

Amaryllis Archer comes into Tash's mind, and she's beautifully lit, and she says, 'That's an extremely good question.' She winks then, and her electric-blue eyeshadow catches the light and is transcendent, just for a moment.

The girls from the attic dorms wait for their turn to be interviewed by DI Archer. They roll around in her eyeline but she does not bob for them; she does not bite into them. Not yet. They don't even know if she has sharp teeth. They plan their interrogation outfits, practise their innocent expressions in the mirror. Take selfies to compare. They raise their eyebrows and lower them again and experiment with the sort of make-up that male teachers can never detect but female ones always can. Not because they plan to lie – not at all – even though they have agreed never to mention the incident with Dr Morgan, or say anything about Bianca. At fifteen you have to practise everything you plan to do. Sitting up in bed, for example, the morning after you've slept with your boyfriend for the first time. What are the angles? Where is the light? How can you look smaller and more precious but with bigger tits? How can you look cool rather than benignly beautiful, and is an ear-cuff the answer?

That afternoon with Nico by the river, with his sister

113

watching. That hadn't ever been practised. If it had been practised, perhaps it would not have happened and Tash could feel purer now because purity is everything.

*

The new biology teacher is called Miss White. She is tall and sporty with thick porridgey calves and short blonde hair. She is going to double-up as a lacrosse and athletics coach. Mr Hendrix has been off sick for ages, so Miss White has agreed to cover some of the history classes as well, with the help of Dr Moone, who lollops more frequently across the grounds now, dragging his bad leg like a puppet pulling its own strings. He up-and-downs and side-to-sides himself past the hedges and the bare branches of the trees and into the Dower House, and tells the girls about the bravery of men in wars, and the cunning things their leaders did.

Miss White never wears make-up. She has a rash on her neck. She hangs leaves on little washing lines to measure how they drip, and grows bacteria in petri dishes and tries, without success, to teach the girls how to use a potometer and Visking tubing.

'Girls,' she says on a dark Tuesday that is oddly warm for January. 'Girls, are there *any* biological things you are interested in? Anything at all? Contraception, for example? Sex? Childbirth? Do you like gory things? Blood? Tropical diseases?'

114

No one says anything. How to tell her that her predecessor has been found dead in the school lake – well, she probably knows that – but how to tell her that, as a result of this, Becky with the bad hair has stopped eating and got her father to write to Dr Moone and ask for Natasha and Tiffanie to be expelled? How to tell her that biology lessons make them feel vertiginous because it turns out that even the most heartless of the girls actually loved Dr Morgan, although of course no one can love him now that he's an actual paedophile? Becky does not believe him to be a paedophile: she believes Tash and Tiffanie to be liars. But all Tash and Tiffanie have said is that they don't think anything happened on the night of the disco. Of course, they've mainly said this to Dominic and Tony, who have extrapolated somewhat and the rumours have gone round, like rumours do. Then there's the question of what actually happened to Bianca. But Bianca was crazy. Bianca probably just walked anorexically past the lake and then slipped anorexically into it.

Poor Dr Morgan. He hasn't even had a funeral yet. He might not have one at all. What if he actually murdered Bianca, and then killed himself out of remorse?

'I know,' says Miss White, clapping her large bony hands together. 'Why don't we look at BMI? Body Mass Index. We can design some experiments. I'll get the scales.'

The girls exchange glances. Miss White cannot know

115

that the girls have not been allowed to weigh themselves since Bianca's death: that all the scales in the school have been hidden from them. It turns out that there is a dusty old set in the biology store-cupboard, which is useful to know about. No one is going to tell her, are they? Nope. Because really, how would you? The mood lifts a little as the day darkens further and the last bits of winter sun dissolve into the clouds and die.

The only people who look uncertain are the fat girls. But even they are sort of excited: excited in that way you are when you know something is going to hurt but you feel compelled to do it anyway. The one person who is genuinely not excited is Rachel. She's recently learned a lot about how to weigh yourself and when. She also knows how it feels if the numbers are even slightly wrong. How damning, how bleak, how painful. How fucking *unfair*, given everything you've done and how hard you've worked and how desperately you want it. At home, her mood for the day is dictated by a number. At least here she's been free of it for a while. What's she going to do if this number is wrong?

'But we've got our clothes on,' she says. 'And it's the middle of the afternoon.'

But it's too late. The scales – large, heavy, dusty – have been brought out and put by the window. From somewhere Miss White has produced a box containing pairs of callipers and now she's demonstrating how you measure someone else's body fat with them. Most of the callipers are white plastic standard-issue, but one pair is metal, old-fashioned and sharp. This is the pair Miss White uses for her demonstration. You have to get hold of someone else's muffin-top and basically pinch it, hard, with these metal things . . .

Is this ethical? Not really. Is it a good idea? No one cares. Miss White has pulled up a table from a Google image search and is displaying it on the biology lab's state-of-the-art projector screen. According to this table, you have to be under 30 per cent fat to be 'normal'. Anything over that is 'obese'. 20–25 per cent is 'slim'. 15–20 per cent is 'athletic'. BMI is different. You don't need callipers for that: you just have to weigh yourself and measure how tall you are and do a simple equation.

Bella puts her hand up.

'Hasn't BMI been discredited?' she says. 'I mean, don't all rugby players come out as horribly obese when it's actually just muscle?'

'Yes, well, that's why we also take body-fat percentages,' says Miss White. 'That way you get a more accurate picture. It's not just rugby players coming up as obese in BMI tests; quite thin-looking people can come out as fat using body-composition methods. Right. Pair up,' she says, 'but not with the same person as usual. Let's mix things up a bit. Yes, good, Bella: you go with Tiffanie. I want everyone's BMI and body-fat percentage entered into this table I'm going to create. Then we can practise using statistics as well.'

Tash ends up with Becky, who sulks the whole time. Her breath is awful from not eating. Is this how her actual insides smell, like rotten egg and antiseptic? When Tash tries to use the callipers on her, Becky simply shakes her off as if she were a stray cat that you have invited in but has started dribbling on you and clawing you too hard.

'Ow!' she says. 'Get off me.'

'Come on, girls,' says Miss White. 'Follow the instructions. You have to release the trigger of the callipers so that the entire force of the jaws is on the skinfold.'

'Why don't you go back to Russia?' Becky says to Tash once Miss White has moved on. 'And stop ruining everything. Go back to your own people and stop bothering us. Like, you have literally destroyed London, my father says so. And it's all with dark money, stolen money. You're basically all criminals.'

Becky refuses to measure Tash, so Tash does the bits she can reach herself, and gets Tiffanie to do the rest. Tiffanie hasn't been able to get any skinfolds from Bella, who doesn't really have any. She is basically zero per cent fat, or something close to it: muscle stretched over wide bones. She also has weird stretch marks, and a sort of dry waxy sheen all over, like a boat in a harbour.

The statistics the class produces are quite a shock, although Rachel is quietly pleased with her own numbers. It turns out that there is a thing called 'skinny fat'. Your BMI might be OK, and that might fool the government,

118

but what if your small body is composed entirely of lard? What if you have literally no muscles, like a veal calf? Tiffanie falls into this category. She has a BMI of 21 but she is 32 per cent fat, which means she is obese.

'Je suis pas *obese*,' she growls, when her stats are pulled off the table as an example. But she looks startled in a way no one has ever seen before. Imagine Tiffanie, with her perfect brown-and-rose body, actually counting as obese. Imagine her now weighing more than Rachel! Later, Miss White will tell some of the other teachers about the class and Madame Vincent will get her to repeat this part again and again and it will give her some small comfort in these dark days after what happened with Dr Morgan.

On the smooth white table in the biology lab, the metal callipers gleam like the hard wet teeth of a praying mantis.

*

It's Wednesday afternoon, and the ballet class is almost over. Miss Annabel has left the room, just for a moment. Occasionally, if the girls have pleased her, she returns from these sorties with an old metal tea-tray holding plastic cups of cold lemonade. But mostly when she leaves the room the girls stop what they're doing and wait to hear the faint squall of water weakly hitting water, and then the long heave of the toilet chain. Miss Annabel

119

pees all the time now. The girls wonder if she is going to die. Today when she goes she accidentally leaves the ballet CD playing, and it somehow gets stuck on a sequence of jumps. They've just done 64 *changements* and some girls – the lazy, obese ones – are now lounging damply by the barre hoping for lemonade. But the more dedicated girls want to keep jumping, and so they do. They jump and jump and the music changes and they bound and scurry for a while and then carry on jumping, this time doing *entrechat quatres*. There was a joke, a long time ago, perhaps even in Year 10, that these jumps, where one calf beats against another four times, were called 'enter shot cats'. Someone remembers this now, and someone else giggles, and the jumping gets wilder, less controlled, and soon the last three girls are staggering around the room, with fingers for guns and/or ears, and they are leaping and dying and meowing and baring their tiny pointed teeth like—

'Girls, for heaven's sake!'

And off they trundle again to the headmaster's office: Tash, Tiffanie and Rachel. Rachel is looking thinner now and people are worried. The headmaster is especially worried, and so he asks her to go to his house, alone, the next day. But for now he simply reads them some more from *Great Expectations* while they breathe in the old-carpet-and-polish smells that are both comforting and hopeless.

*

It has come to the teachers' attention that anorexia is on the rampage again, despite everyone's best efforts and the programme of talks. Even Becky with the bad hair has succumbed. Her hipbones have started jutting out of her skirt like a cowboy's thumbs, and she doesn't even seem to care about being Head Girl any more. No one eats anything, at least not in public. Those who must eat follow Rachel, who only eats fish and vegetables. Rachel has started photocopying sheets of exercises and her rules for 'clean eating' and selling them to the crushlets for £1 each. You can do triceps dips on the big enamel baths, and press-ups on the bathroom floor. You can lock yourself in and do twenty-one minutes' worth of plyometrics when other people think you're doing a poo. If you do it right you'll only need to poo every three days, and you won't have periods either, which is handy in a boarding school. Tiffanie has stopped eating carbs and is losing some of her fat, but it doesn't suit her to be so pinched and wrinkled. Her hair is less shiny. She's like a pedigree dog with worms, or an apple that someone left in the sun and then forgot to eat.

It's all becoming a bit much for the teachers. The scales are hidden yet again. The callipers are removed. The headmaster gives Miss White a talking-to about what an appropriate biology lesson should be. At supper the Year 11 girls are split up. Surely there can be no more competitive non-eating if they cannot see each other. So Tash is next to Sin-Jin, who has tea-stained teeth and frequently eats with her mouth open. The meatsmell from the teachers' plates is disgusting. All Tash wants to smell are flowers and perfumes and English cigarette smoke. The rest of the dining hall is thick with the stench of fat and treacle and Miss Annabel's bunion cream and the haemorrhoid gel that Madame Vincent no doubt uses. Often in the mornings the headmaster's study smells of dark coffee and tobacco, and that has become the scent of Estella. Pip would not eat custard like this, or love someone who did. Estella does not eat in the entire book and she does not die, because she is glorious, and she can live on Pip's love. She certainly never eats treacle tart.

In the dorms, in the dayless murk of early evening WiFi, the girls share links to sites that explain 'skinny fat'. Most of these sites have pictures of soft pretty girls that look like Tash and Tiffanie next to pictures of girls that look more like something you'd find if you searched for #thighgap on Instagram. The former is wrong and the latter is correct. Site after site confirms this. After all, who wants to be fat and look thin? Or, at least, who can kid themselves that they look thin when they are a massive UK size 8 and everyone wants to be a US size 00?

Tash gets an email from Weight Watchers inviting her to a meeting in the village. She hasn't lost any weight in the last two weeks and the website wonders if she needs extra help. Perhaps she does. She can go after supper on Monday. They will have scales there. She can be weighed in. Start afresh. Try to look more like the *after* pictures than the *before* ones. Although frankly some – most – of the *after* pictures are not even that attractive. But it's not about being attractive. It's about winning. Tash probably won't win, but at least she's still in the running. She fantasises about actually repulsing Nico. She imagines him running his finger up and down her torso like he did that time, but now with the aim of arriving at her breasts or her knicker-line totally ruined by the hardness and reality of her ribcage, like those dinosaurs at the museum.

On Sunday night the girls break out of the attic dorms and it's like an Enid Blyton book except it isn't because in what Enid Blyton book do girls escape at midnight to weigh themselves on kitchen scales that they then break? It's Tiffanie, of course. Her obese lardarse. The kitchen full of food but no one eating any of it. No normal midnight-feast behaviour here. Except that Tiffanie *may* have pocketed some treacle tart when no one was looking, because it doesn't matter now that she's not even in the competition. Rachel is still winning. Who even knew she had it in her? And Becky with the bad hair coming from the outside like some kind of blinkered grey gelding with trust issues. Although she probably won't be able to overtake at this point, and it looks like Rachel will be the next Head Girl.

You can't weigh yourself on Google either, in case you were wondering.

On Monday after prep, Rachel goes for her secret run and Tash sneaks off to the village. She has a Weight Watchers gold membership card already: something to do with the black Amex perhaps, or just how thin she is compared to most people on Weight Watchers. No one here has ever seen a gold membership card before. They have never had anyone here who weighs as little as Tash does, with her BMI bordering on underweight. They have never seen a coat like this one, a handbag like that. She smells of hothouse orchids and sultry youth and clean, just-made flesh, that babysmell still somewhere in the mix. She is everything they will never be again, not ever. When she weighs in everyone claps, and some of the women weep. When she leaves, one of the organisers asks if she can touch her, just her arm, just because. It is as if they have been visited by an angel.

Tash can't help it; she tells the other bad apples about her trip to the village and soon they are all going. First Tiffanie, who obviously really needs it, and then Lissa and then Donya, Dani and even Rachel, who says it is simply research. Everyone signs up for the meetings online and then they head to the village in little clusters in their school cloaks. Perhaps Rachel is the last straw, with her abs and those spring-chicken triceps. The angels have become an infestation and the fat village ladies, the mothers of the village boys and the stable girls, don't like it any more. They are overrun with thin glorious beauty and they can't fucking stand it. It is one thing

124

having a picture on your fridge; it is quite another having this perfect flesh pushed in your face day after day after day. They lock up their sons. They complain to the school. The punishments and talks begin again. The headmaster brings in a girl in a wheelchair whose organs almost failed when she was anorexic. The girl is called Jacqueline. Her hair is the skin of a freshly picked aubergine and she is all yin, all nightshade. She is still sneaky too; you can tell by the way she moves her little hands.

The headmaster himself wheels her from the car that delivers her into the school, and then back out again. Someone inside the car is helping, but it looks as if he tips her in, like a pile of apples falling from a wheelbarrow: like a dead body.

It's too late anyway. Becky with the bad hair gets sent home, and then to some sort of clinic. Imagine: if this can happen to Becky, it can happen to literally anyone. When she returns, they all start calling her Jackie, and then Jack.

'You are a dangerous little group of replicating cells,' says Madame Vincent. 'You girls are a cancer in this school. What about the juniors, who look up to you?'

Becky with the bad hair won't embrace the name Jack, so Lissa takes it instead. She's in the race suddenly now too, because being sent home is so magnificent and dreadful. If she can get in real trouble, like getting-sent-home trouble, then her mother will surely notice her and stop thinking only about Douglas. And Suze needs her sister. She has been singing in a country and western band, even though she can't really sing, and goes around Cambridge at all hours wearing shoplifted miniskirts and cowboy boots. She came home with a black eye the other week, after a long weird night with Danny, the other vocalist in the band. He did it because he was drunk, and because Suze didn't like his new song, and because she had raised his hopes only to dash them.

Tiffanie will now only respond to the name Stan, which is a strange French shortening of Estella. Dani has become Beau: like Beauty in *Beauty and the Beast*, but disguised as a mortal man. Donya started as Sonja, because it rhymed, and because the girls still lap up all the stories about Aunt Sonja that Tash brings back: stories of castles and diets and elegantly poached fish. Then Donya became simply Sonj, with that weird foreign J that everyone loves to say even though you're not supposed to, but now she is just Son or Sonny. Tash is sometimes Princess Augusta, shortened to Goose or even, more frequently now, Gus.

They are all in disguise. This is important. They have code-names.

The infestation of angels now moves on to the church. It is another punishment, one not appreciated by the village vicar, who believes religion is many things but not this. The mothers of the village boys turn up to look, and nudge, and complain, and so the flock is massive, for two weeks only. Far bigger than the turnout for Dr

Morgan's funeral, which was attended in the end only by Dr Moone, Sin-Jin and Miss Annabel. The angels flutter now in their green cloaks and roost in the gallery above the main congregation. Natasha – today Tash, Moustache, Mustafa, Muskrat, Muscles, because she has always had strong arms after all – looks down at the women with their pig-leg limbs, their thighs bigger, surely, than any body part on any known creature, and she prays for them once more. *Dear God*, she says, earnestly, in her head. *Dear God, please bless these ladies and remove fat from them, oh God. Let them feel beautiful and in this feeling release them from fat and the discomfort they must surely feel when they have to take off their clothes in front of their husbands, or have a bath.* Afterwards she is not sure if she said this prayer in English or Russian and she goes back to the Hail Mary in French, because it is so comforting.

On the way out of church one of the Weight Watchers women seems to wait for her. This woman is big – they all are – with breasts like permanent crossed arms under her cheap supermarket clothes. Her weather-beaten face hangs in elephantine folds around a pair of massive, unattractive glasses. Yet there is something beautiful about her that Tash can't quite fathom. Some vague wisdom in her eyes. But there is more in the eyes too: swirled about in the wisdom is envy and resignation and something important. Knowledge.

'So,' says the woman. 'I just wanted you to know that I didn't agree with what the others did, and I said so.

127

You're always welcome in the village as far as I'm concerned.'

'Thank you,' says Tash. 'But what do you mean?'

'When Weight Watchers banned you all.'

'Oh. Well, our school banned us first, so.' Tash shrugs.

'What's your name, girlie?'

'Gus.'

'*Gus?*'

'Short for Augusta.'

'Like the princess?'

'Yes. Exactly like that.'

The woman sighs for a long time. 'He did it to his wife,' she says. 'And now he's systematically doing it to the whole school. Don't your mothers care?'

The way she says *systematically* is interesting from a language point of view. It's a long, complex word that she quite brutally glottal-stops right in the middle. She jabs her finger in the direction of the school just at the moment of the glottal stop.

'Sorry? Who?'

'Your headmaster,' says the woman. 'That's who.'

The others have already gone on ahead. On the way back Tash searches alone for the little grave, amongst the sharp green erections of the late-spring flowers. Was it here, down this narrow path? Was it nearer the fountain? Eventually she finds it down a half-hidden track behind the horse sculpture, in a spot from which you can look back over the lake to the school buildings beyond.

The stone has been recently cleaned, and someone has put a simple bunch of freesias in front of it, using a jam jar as a vase.

*

The slam book comes back, and at first no one can remember what it even is, this thick, bulging hardback notebook laminated in plastic. Wait. Was it actually laminated in plastic before or . . . Did the boys at Harrow do that? How sweet. How quaint. How—

'Whose idea exactly was this?' asks Miss White. She's turning the book over in her hands like it's something about to be sent off to be decontaminated, or possibly blown up, like those elderly ladies' handbags from the olden days when they used to leave them in Boots and people thought they might contain a bomb. Now, of course, people are more careful, and strap bombs to themselves. Nowadays nobody puts them in elderly ladies' handbags – or in slam books, for that matter.

'Mr Hendrix,' says Bella.

'It was actually my idea,' says Donya.

'No, it wasn't,' says Elle sourly. 'It was Bianca's.'

Everyone is so veryvery grumpy. Having a light body has not translated into having a light heart. Indeed, these bodies can no longer contain these hearts. Tiffanie has not cried in five years but now she is tearful all the time, and her tears get stuck in her new wrinkles like blobs of

129

shark oil. Lissa sighs a lot and says bitchy things. She points out Rachel's remaining backfat, for example. The cellulite under her bum cheeks. Dani isn't speaking to her parents. Donya has started reading the weird books about radical Islam sent by her sexy cousin, but even then the words sort of blur, and it's all so tiring.

Putting your calories into MyFitnessPal every evening takes such a long time and is laborious and depressing. Rachel has been on at them all to *not* put in what they've eaten today retrospectively but to use the app to plan what they're going to eat tomorrow and stick to it. Everyone is friends with everyone on MyFitnessPal, even people they don't like, even Becky with the bad hair. Rachel is also friends with Jordon and, through him, the twins Millie and Izzy, and some of the other fitness instructors at the gym. She can see what Jordon eats in a day. It makes her feel close to him. He never writes to her – he says writing isn't really his thing – but he does 'like' every weight loss she puts into the system. He eats a lot of protein powder and egg whites and cottage cheese.

Everyone has sort of flopped. They are hanging over their chairs like old coats; like drunks in a Munch painting. It's almost four o'clock and there's nothing to look forward to. The school has stopped providing afternoon tea because literally no one eats it. Instead, prep begins early. Then music lessons, or drama. Then fish and vege-tables. Then MyFitnessPal, then bed. No one even likes music or drama any more because they seem to come from another dimension entirely, an irrelevant, lost life that the girls are no longer living. They are hungry ghosts, flickering on the edge of this world.

But now this. The slam book. Filled with pictures of unknown boys, and their responses to the girls' questionnaires, and – importantly – a bit where each one has ranked the girls in order of who they fancy most, and in which Zoe does surprisingly well, despite being fat. Is it her skin? Her pretty face? But no one knows of this treasure just yet, because Miss White won't give it to them. She thinks it's inappropriate. Rachel has to spend three hours at the headmaster's house before he agrees to talk to Miss White about it. Rachel comes back from this sortie glowing with pre-Head Girlness and a sort of clandestine power. She has learned other things. For example, everyone thought that Mr Hendrix had been banned from the school for some creepy and disturbing reason connected with Dr Morgan, and possibly men in general, but it isn't that. The headmaster has hinted of a 'dark secret', something not many of the girls know about, and he's told Rachel to never mention this, but after lights-out she asks them all, and Tash says it might be about her and Tiffanie and the photographs that do not exist. The ones taken by Dr Morgan, the paedophile who then killed himself.

No one can remember now why these facts were supposed to be concealed, and so Tash and Tiffanie tell all about what is supposed to have happened on the Malibu night and how they don't remember it but are still nevertheless victims of abuse.

They try to remember what happened to Amaryllis Archer.

The following day the slam book is there in the Year 11 common room. The apples manage to grab it before Becky with the bad hair even knows it's there.

What you need to know about Bianca, writes Bianca's twin, Caleb, who does exist, albino-looking and weird in his photo like a grounded fledgling. *What you need to know about Bianca is* . . . And then whatever Caleb wrote has been Tippexed out. The girls chip away at the Tippex with their compass points, but underneath is just scribble. Who has done this? What on earth was he trying to say?

*

It's not food poisoning. No one eats food, so no one is likely to be poisoned by it. It's a virus. A vomiting virus. It strikes the hockey team first. Did they catch it from their last away game, to that hideous concrete pleb school on the other side of Stevenage where the other girls sledged them by saying that their parents don't love them, because how could they if they sent them to boarding school? Were the germs maybe on the ball? In the mud? In the other girls' stringy hair? Their melancholy pubes? No one knows.

It had been an upsetting game not just because they were beaten by the plebs, the Emilys and Hannahs – the utter indignity – but also because of the dark figure on the sidelines, a sexy teacher in a leather jacket, a teacher known by these boarding-school girls to have his ex-girlfriend's name tattooed on his chest, and the words *Fail Better* on his upper arm. A teacher not belonging to them any more, but now belonging to the plebs, as if they didn't already have everything: homes with parents who actually care, who even occasionally go with them to Topshop on a Saturday and then buy them lunch at EAT or Pret.

Not that anyone can think about food now. The hockey players are all in the same dorm, luckily, the vast rectangular sunlit one on the first floor. It's the biggest dorm in the school, always occupied by those stupid-but-happy girls with lots of friends who prefer being in crowds: team players, leaders, followers, extroverts. They all have bouncy hair. The beds in this dorm have not been slept in by dead girls and do not carry faint stains of periods and dusty bits of old sherbet. These girls make sure they change their sheets regularly. They know how to put duvet covers on. Their parents send them pink throws and hot-water bottles with knitted covers. In this dorm are teddy bears and medals and little trophies and hair-brushes with the big matted clumps of hair removed from them and not put in another girl's bed, or set fire to, but simply thrown away.

And now the dorm contains buckets filled with yellow puke.

A sour smell everywhere. The girls are hot, sososo hot, and then cold, sososo cold, and their limbs ache and actually is it possible to just take off your arms and legs and could someone please come and suck the heavy rancid stuff out of their brains and – woah – sitting up is too much effort and vomiting on the floor by the bucket is actually a great achievement considering, and anyway no one cares and everyone wants to die.

This is literally the worst thing that has happened to anybody. If they had the choice, right now, between being mildly sexually abused by a dead biology teacher and this, days more of this, this pukey, churny, constant nausea and weakness worse than the wilted parsley Mrs Cuckoo sometimes puts on the steamed fish, they'd take the first one: the painless photos, the slight smoothing of the sheets in such a way that—

'What smoothing?' Tash had asked Dominic. 'I still don't understand what is supposed to have happened. There wasn't any "smoothing".'

'What about rubbing?' he'd asked. 'Was there any rubbing?'

Anyway, even moderate sexual abuse would be better than this. Anything would. All pleasure in life is gone. The joy of eating went a long time ago, of course, but now there is not even joy in starving. Those narcotic feelings of missing a couple of meals have been replaced by a general feeling that existence is entirely without purpose. No one can read. No one wants to listen to music. No one has a future. Everything is pointless.

*

Only Rachel, with her staggering new immune system and her fresh gut, full of probiotics and little helpful creatures and gumption, does not succumb to the sickness bug. Is it because she spends so much time outside? Is it because she is essentially perfect now? Of course, the vomiting has made the others lose astonishing amounts of weight, apparently, but Rachel can't see any of her friends to find out more. They are in quarantine, lying on camp beds in between the real beds of the hockey team, being puked on occasionally by Bella and Elle and Becky with the bad hair. It's like a WWI sanatorium in there. Spanish flu. Death. Amputations. Cheerful nurses in crisp uniforms, except . . . There are no nurses. Occasionally Sin-Jin looks in, an embroidered handkerchief pressed over her face. Miss Annabel doesn't go near the first floor, let alone the dorm. Miss White managed to visit once and swore – out loud – and then her face turned the colour first of the puke and then of ghosts and so someone told the headmaster that they'd need agency nurses but the school matron said not to be so silly and she'd come and get the buckets when she had a moment.

The crushlets are sent home. Year 10 is sent home. The only girls left in the school are the ones with the virus, and Rachel. It's like a zombie film, or it would be if anyone had ever seen one. Also, if it were a zombie film then Rachel, the one surviving humanoid (teachers obviously don't count), would presumably have to rescue someone or do something heroic but she's far too busy for any of that.

'Come on,' says Miss White to Rachel. 'There's no reason why we can't do PE on our own. What do you want to do? Javelin? Long jump? Sports Day's coming and you must want to win something? Let's train you up. One to one.'

Rachel runs a fast hundred metres, and then two hundred metres and then a 5K. Miss White wonders about a heptathlon or a decathlon. Can Rachel throw? Nope. Can she jump. Yes. Yes – Rachel really can jump. Now she's not fat, she can snake her body like a bendy piece of liquorice up and over the bar of the high jump, no matter how high Miss White raises it. And the thick mat is there each time like a massive waterproof sponge. Thwack, wriggle, up-and-over, thwack, wriggle . . . Until the time when the thick plastic blue mat just isn't there any more, when Rachel somehow overshoots, misses and lands on her arm. Thwack, ow, fuckfuckfuck.

So now Matron is busy with Rachel and her broken arm in sick bay and the buckets go uncollected for hours. For a whole day. Zoe and Ayesha recover enough to get some slightly stale chocolate logs from their trunks and no one's exactly stopping them and they binge-eat them and then immediately throw them up again, the thick brown puke adding interest to the custardy bile that is all anyone has managed to produce for days.

Eventually Matron comes and removes all the remaining food from the dorm and the girls are put on a starvation diet. It's the only thing for a vomiting epidemic; everyone should know that. You starve until there's nothing to come up any more, not even bile: only then are you cured. Only then can the thing no longer be spread. You go two days beyond that point, even when the patients beg you for food, just to be sure. Each day someone brings a 12-pack of Evian and dumps it in the dorm like a massive bunch of bananas being delivered to a gorilla's cage. Then they lock the door. Or they may as well.

In a haze of painkillers and late-spring sunshine Rachel sleeps in the best sick-bay bed and dreams she is fat again. She remembers her moustache. Platefuls of potatoes. Cheese sandwiches. Dr Moone is looking at her again and writing down her measurements and explaining how important it is for women to be elegant and beautiful, and that norms, non-aesthetes, haters, plebs – these people from the outside will say you're too skinny, but that's not actually possible. He shows her that book again, his hardback of black and white photographs of Grace Kelly. That is the ideal, he says.

137

This is the kind of thing humans must aspire to. Not men, who are lost forever after the Fall, but women, by nature far closer both to angels and forest creatures, who can save us all with their pure beauty. He reads to her from Coleridge: 'Oft she said, "I'm not grown thin!" and then her wrist she spann'd'. He expounds, as usual, on his theory of asthenics, where bodies must be lean, breastless, taut. The dream dissolves into Rachel accidentally ordering a slice of chocolate cake in a café – the same café they went to on the Cambridge trip – and it being served with whipped cream. Rachel is trying to say no to the cake and the cream but she's lost her voice and . . .

She wakes up sweating, with damp sheets. But it's OK. There was never any chocolate cake. Rachel sits up and breathes, and when she finds Matron is not there she sneaks into the sick-bay office and weighs herself. It's OK. Nothing has changed. It's fine. The box is safe. Rachel sees her life now as a small, rectangular glass box, and in the box is everything of importance to her, tidily arranged. There's her gym plan, her school exercise plan, her records on MyFitnessPal. How clean and neat it all is. Nothing else matters. She thinks of the twins with their perfect bodies and how they are nothing more than that but how wonderful it is: to be just body, just pure. Why would you need exams? Well, except the ones to become a personal trainer, which is what Rachel is going to be. She imagines herself with her clients in the sunshine in a park, doing bootcamps. Then it's the summer and she is toned and brown, unlike her worst clients, and there she is on a beach with Jordon, with one of those bikinis that fit in the crack of your bum, and she has her navel piercing and he turns to her with his deep blue eyes and says—

'Why are you out of bed, missy?'

'I've only got a broken arm,' says Rachel. 'I don't see why I have to stay here.'

'It's just until your mother can come and collect you,' says Matron.

'Why can't I go back to my dorm?'

'They're cleaning everything out, after this norovirus or whatever they decide it is. Anyway, I want you where I can see you. Make sure you're eating.'

'I thought everyone had been banned from eating.'

'Ha, yes, well, that would suit you, wouldn't it?'

Matron is about as far away from Grace Kelly as you can get without being a man. Although she may as well be a man. She is vast, un-made-up, hairy. She is sexless, like a dough-ball. From her neck to her knees, a zone that should be all interest and angles and light and shade, there is just one great milky mass, like a boring hike on the moon.

'You know diets don't work?' she says to Rachel. 'It's all a big con.'

Rachel rolls her eyes. She holds her glass box close to her. Says nothing.

'Diets make you put on weight in the long run,' she says. 'I don't suppose your fancy-pants magazines tell you that, though.'

'Doesn't sound very scientific,' says Rachel.

'No? Well, what would I know? I've only been a nurse all my life.'

'If dieting doesn't work, then why is everyone so thin?'

'What, your friends?' Matron cackles. 'They're fifteen. Everyone's thin at fifteen. Well, except you, of course. You were properly chubby. May have just been puppy fat, who knows? Anyway, now you're thin because you've been on a diet. So next time you get fat, you'll be fatter than before. That's how it works.'

'I won't get fat again,' says Rachel. 'That's ridiculous.'

'Is it?'

'Anyway, I know you're a nurse and everything, but—'

'But what?' Matron raises her eyebrows.

Rachel shrugs. 'I just . . .'

'I've been dieting all my life, love. And look where it's got me.'

'What about Grace Kelly?' says Rachel. 'And Kate Moss?'

'They're not like us, darling,' says Matron, and winks.

*

At the height of the savagery, when the naked starving girls are left for hours and hours with their buckets

140

unchanged, with no WiFi, no food, no clean clothes, no nothing – not even any village boys baying at the windows for sex – someone takes a series of photographs. It's disgusting when you think about it, what goes on in these institutions. Someone should do an exposé. These poor skinny wretches so forsaken, flesh-fallen and alone.

But when Suze sends the pictures to the tabloids all she gets back are brief notes saying 'no thanks' and 'not for us' and 'to be honest, love, our readers don't care what happens to toffs' children in their elitist schools'.

'Oh well,' she says to Lissa. 'I tried.'

They are mucking out the ponies. When Lissa isn't here a woman from the village helps, and her daughter rides Lissa's pony, Apple. When Lissa is here the daughter cries and the mother has one slice of toast in the morning instead of two. Suze didn't ride Plum for years but now here she is again with her hair in a long plait wearing a check shirt and no make-up.

'What happened with your teacher?' asks Suze. 'The one who died?'

Lissa shrugs. 'No one really knows. He was probably a paedophile.'

'Fucking hell. These fucking schools.' Suze shakes her head.

'Yeah, well,' says Lissa. 'Literally no one cares.'

Suze went to a local day school. But by the time it was Lissa's turn their parents had split up and their mother had to travel so much more and there just wasn't anyone at home for weeks on end; well, except Suze and her boyfriends. There was the memorable year they dropped acid and watched *The Silence of the Lambs* while the house flooded and no one did anything. The year they set fire to the thatch of the village shop. The year one of the boyfriends got kicked almost to death by one of the ponies, which actually served him right.

And now Suze is getting married to one of them. The one who gave her the black eye. This is what they've come out to the stables to talk about. It's not that Suze needs Lissa's blessing exactly, but it's clear that there's something to explain. Specifically, why is Suze going to leave Lissa for a violent psychopath who actually – last time Lissa checked – lives in a fucking bungalow with his mother in one of the drab villages on the other side of Cambridge?

'It was literally a one-off,' says Suze, about the black eye. 'I mean, I punched him too that night.'

'Mum says—'

'Yeah, like Mum knows all about relationships.'

Lissa winces. If she could just manage to get hospitalised before the wedding . . . ? But she doesn't have the willpower of some of the others. Becky with the bad hair has it but then she does all that sport, all that no-pain, no-gain stuff. Lissa is still too partial to chocolate, and lemon sweets, and the half-eaten tube of Polos she always carries for the ponies. Even if you skip lunch and never eat pudding these things add up. And also if you like to

142

eat crisps when you're sad and lonely. She's not really got skin in this game.

'Anyway,' says Suze. 'I'm having an engagement party, and you can invite all your friends.'

'Really? Will there be boys?'

'Oh yes.'

'Well . . .'

'We'll get wasted. It'll be great.'

*

At Aunt Sonja's, Tash is having trouble getting out of bed. She's fine now, really she is. Like, she *can* actually get out of bed without puking or passing out. She has even started eating again. That last day of the sickness at school, when all the remaining girls were told to go down to the dining room, and it was oddly cold and light and echoey and Mrs Cuckoo brought them each a mug of either Marmite or Bovril and one slice of dry white bread and some of the girls cried and some stuffed the whole piece of bread in their mouths and then tried to bargain with other girls for their slices. Some picked the crust off first and then ate it in little pieces, delicately, soberly.

Not one person left a single crumb.

Before that, Miss White had insisted on weighing them, because the whole thing had accidentally created a very impressive set of stats that she might be able to use in some way, possibly in collaboration with Dr Moone. And indeed, Year 11 had, during the sickness episode, lost a total of ten stone: the equivalent of one whole girl (admittedly quite a large one).

Again, the tabloids wrote back with disdain. 'So it possibly could be a story, that your posh, upper-class, oligarch bitches had mass bulimia so bad that someone actually *died*, but that's not what happened, is it? Your cosseted girls just had an ordinary sickness bug, probably caught from one of our competitors' readers, and no one died, because the weight of a person is not a person and if you think our honest readers want to hear about your fat-cat science experiment then you're fucking deluded.'

Or words to that effect.

That last hour before they left for home, all the photos of them in their too-big skirts like a photoshoot for the next generation of supermodels. And now everyone is bouncing back. Dry toast quickly became toast with butter, which became toast with butter and jam, which became full roast dinners and big sighs of relief from all the parents, or at least the ones who care, and the whole chapter fading into history except . . .

Tash does not know what to eat. She does not know what to eat, and she does not know what to wear, and she does not know what to do. This is why she can't get up. As long as she stays in bed everything's on hold. Even breakfast. What does a normal person have for breakfast?

Does a normal person even have breakfast? Anastasia's book recommends fasting for as long as you can overnight: ideally having your dinner at 5 or 6 p.m. and then not eating again until lunch the next day. Tash can't remember why. Something to do with giving your digestive system a rest and preventing bloating? Because who wants to be bloated, right? But then everything else you read about being healthy says to eat breakfast. Eat oats. Except don't oats contain those thingummies that make you fat and mad?

All the conversations the girls have had about food. All the diets. Rachel's factsheets. You put them together and there's nothing left. There is literally nothing anyone can eat. Maybe broccoli and other green vegetables. That's it. Everything else is a violation of something. And Tash does not have an objective any more. That's the other problem. Does she even want to be thin? Well, yes, of course: don't all girls want to be thin? But, OK, wait: what if she was fat instead? What if she was fat and invisible with her special adipose shield that would prevent any other abuser from getting anywhere near her?

That was what Dominic said in their last session before the sickness.

'You put on a few pounds, girlie? Trying to keep the wolves at bay?'

It was true, but the main reason was Tiffanie and her sudden espousal of food: expensive chocolates sent from

Paris, and vast filled loaves from the village shop; whole white bloomers cut and stuffed with an entire packet of cheese and half a jar of Hellman's and a massive dollop of Branston. One for everyone!

Dominic told Tash all about butch lesbians who hate men and keep them away with their actual bodies. Their ballast. Their fearsomeness. The beards they grow from the testosterone produced by spending all their time thinking about fannies.

Has anyone written to the tabloids about Dominic? Perhaps. But they probably wouldn't be interested in him, either. After all, what's he really done? Tried to help a few pretty girls be less mad. That's not a crime, is it?

'I don't hate men,' Tash had said. But was that strictly true? She hates Nico, after all. And Teddy Ross, probably. And of course Dominic and Tony. Dr Moone has started creeping her out a bit. But she loves her father, and Mr Hendrix is quite nice too, not that she has seen either of them for ages.

'It's natural when you're a victim of abuse,' said Dominic. The way he said the word, Tash remembers, makes it sound like *amuse*. You are a victim of *amuse*.

'What is?'

'You either become afraid of men, or you become a total slag and throw yourself at them. But once you get to that stage you're totally fucked up. You need to treat the root cause before then. Dig out the decay before it can spread.'

146

'Literally nothing happened,' said Tash. Or maybe she didn't. Hadn't she stopped saying that by then, given that it never had any effect on Dominic? Wasn't she just waiting by then for him to give up and go away? Hadn't she just resigned herself to the fact that she had been abused, ruined, ravaged, and it was actually worse because she did not remember it? Her innocence gone. Her life over. Chipped, tarnished, broken. Her past dragging behind her like Dr Moone's leg.

Being pure means you can think straight. Being one of the abused means something quite different. How can you ever relax if you've been abused? Can you be happy? Nope. Happiness in the abused is at best a sort of hysteria, a mania, an emotional quelling. It shows you have not fully appreciated the gravity of what has happened to you. So how should a victim be? A victim should definitely wear sombre, or possibly extreme, clothes, should never have fun, should cry during any future sexual encounter, should feel scarred at all times . . .

But should victims eat breakfast?

Tash puts her head back under the covers. Soon she hears the quiet click of the door closing. Aunt Sonja, off to work. Aunt Sonja, who said that time you should only eat fruit in the mornings but has changed her mind recently and has a single poached egg on a wholewheat muffin. Maybe Tash should just do that. Maybe . . . She closes her eyes and sees Princess Augusta with her harp between her large legs. Princess Augusta being ravaged by the sultan. Princess Augusta's pure love for Sir Brent Spencer. But does anyone truly know anything about Princess Augusta? After being ravaged by the sultan, did Princess Augusta feel like a victim? Might she have been fascinated instead? Might she have actually ravaged *him*? She could have left him bleeding and afraid, or just deli-quescent and rapt, whispering in his hoarse hopeless voice that he loves her, loves her above all others, that he will die for her a thousand times, as she laughs cruelly at him and goes back to Sir Brent as if nothing has happened.

And what did she eat for breakfast the next morning?

Tash stands up slowly and puts on her dressing gown. She goes to the sunlit kitchen and stares at the Thames, pulsing as it always does, not caring whether its traffic is party boats or commercial barges or little ferries going between art galleries. The fluorescence shining only on the pure today, because perhaps the fluorescence has a sense of humour, or perhaps it is all subjective anyway.

Her trunk is still there in the hallway. She has not yet unpacked it.

Tash eats an egg on a muffin and feels relieved. One meal down: two to go. If she could just get past this and into . . . What? The Life of the Abused. She sighs. Thinks of home. All the ravaged ladies together in one place with their washing machine cycles and their soap operas. Babies and takeaways. People shouting at each other, but always about the wrong things. No one living for beauty. Because who can?

The life of the amused.

After breakfast she has a shower and then opens her trunk. And there it is. The slam book. Tiffanie said Tash should have it, because she was the only one going back to London. *London,* where the fluorescence shines brightest, and where it now carefully picks out Natasha through the window and bathes her in a complex veily light, and welcomes her back in, because whoever is in London is the one who has to go and see Caleb and find out what the fuck was under the Tippex.

*

It seems that insurgent, nihilist genes run in the Downlowe family, because Caleb, like Bianca, put a false mobile phone number in the slam book. When Tash dials it she gets a pissed-off man in a kebab shop in Ladbroke Grove.

Well, that's that then. Tash can spend the rest of the day on the Piccadilly Line again, although the thought now bores her. She's not really that person any more. Perhaps she can just go walking along the river, see an art exhibition. Maybe something made from elephant dung or refugees' blood. She has to find some way to show Aunt Sonja that she is OK; that she doesn't have to go to some terrible clinic full of Dominics and Tonys. Tash is not confident that she has properly conveyed the facts, i.e. that the sickness was a bug, a quirk of germs and biology, and now the whole school is closed until

149

after Easter. It was uncertain at dinner last night. In fact, Natasha hadn't liked the shift in mood, the different way Aunt Sonja looked at her, as if she was a victim of something.

Doesn't Teddy Ross go to Harrow? Tash has *his* number.

After the dinner in the castle on Boxing Day, and once the elderly ladies had gone to bed, the young people, including the real prostitutes, retired to the drawing room. The freckled boy and his friends snorted cocaine off the covers of first editions of Evelyn Waugh novels while Natasha drank fresh mint tea and then pretended to look at the bookcases. Before she went up to bed, Teddy had come over to her. She'd noticed that he hadn't been doing any coke either. Instead, he'd been sitting silently on the ancient-looking sofa with a cigar and a small crystal tumbler of Cointreau.

'Do you like Cointreau?' he'd asked her, standing a little too close so their arms were touching. He smelled triply of boy and man and animal.

She'd shrugged.

'Try some,' he'd said, offering her his glass. 'I don't mind the lipstick.'

It was warm, so warm, and perfectly orangepeely. Tash took another sip and then gave the glass back.

'Do you like it?'

She'd nodded.

'Do you want to sleep with me?'

'Not now,' she'd said, after a pause. Something in the Cointreau mingled with the dessert wine she'd liked despite saying she'd never drink again, and all the brandy in the trifle, and she felt firelit and comfortable and so she'd grinned at Teddy and touched his arm lightly. 'Wait till we're married,' she'd said.

The next morning when the helicopter had come to get them it had been grey and drizzling, and there had been no sign of her father at all. The butler had run out of the side door, slipping a little on the wet ground, and Natasha thought he was coming to stop them, perhaps because they'd just had a call from her father who was on his way and—

But instead he'd handed her a piece of blue Smythson paper with a phone number on it, slightly smeared from the rain, but still legible.

'From Teddy,' he'd said.

Should Natasha send Teddy a message now? If she does, will she have to sleep with him? Does she want to? Could she just ask for Caleb's number straight out, or will that sound wrong, like she wants to sleep with Caleb instead? Should she have already contacted Teddy? After all, it was months ago that he gave her his number. Natasha imagines Aunt Sonja's face at dinner if she hears not only that the investigation is under way once more, but that Tash has actually done something for her father, for the family. Because she was supposed to like Teddy, right? Tash still hasn't seen her father. He is apparently

151

at the property in France, and will send for her in the summer.

If Tash had to actually marry Teddy in order to be accepted into her father's world, would she? Of course. She would do almost anything. She has a feeling she won't care much for this world, but he is her father. It would be good to get sex over with, with someone real. And anything beats returning to her mother's orbit, which is damp and flea-bitten and hard, and where Nico and his sister still sleep on bare mattresses with only the family dog for warmth. Nico's fat mother has nothing, which explains it. But Natasha's mother keeps two ivory silk pillowcases for herself while Natasha has a single stained pillow that has never had a case and has never been washed.

Tash puts Teddy's number into WhatsApp and composes a brief message. *So our school has been condemned and I'm in London. Maybe let's have coffee somewhere central?*

It sounds more sophisticated than she feels.

It'll have to be in Harrow, comes back the reply, almost immediately. *I've got Theology and Philosophy this afternoon.*

Tash messages Tiffanie in Paris, telling her that she won't believe what she's done, and for the rest of the morning there is this nice back and forth, mainly in French, with Tiffanie wanting to know what underwear Tash is planning to wear, and Tash saying she's sure it doesn't matter because she's not going to sleep with Teddy and anyway she can't because he has Theology and Philosophy. Tiffanie says that if you let on to a man that you're wearing stockings he will give up literally anything and go to bed with you. You can tell him directly (possibly pretending it is a joke), or just drop hints, or you can just let a little bit of the tops show if you are feeling bold, although of course he may then mistake you for a whore.

Tash then reminding Tiffanie that she's only going to see Teddy to get Caleb's number so she can find out what was under the Tippex, like she promised. *What you need to know about Bianca is . . .* What?

Harrow-on-the-Hill is like going back in history, into one of those old-timey British novels that Tash has never read but knows exist. Like those books they were snorting coke off on Boxing Day, maybe. It's all red brick and moss and old gravestones and lichens. Teddy is waiting for her in a café near the church. He doesn't look the way she remembers him. He is paler, but also slightly freckled. His nose turns up a little. He is halfway through a double espresso, and looks slightly too big for the dainty table for two by the window looking out onto the graveyard.

He stands up when he sees her. Tells her where to sit. Orders her a macchiato.

'So,' he says. 'You've come to see me.'

There is no Cointreau here. Tash feels faintly repulsed by him, more than she expected to be. But she is repulsed by Nico now too. Maybe she is becoming a lesbian, like Dominic predicted. Maybe all men will repulse her soon.

153

'Do you want a cake?' Teddy asks her.

'No thanks.'

'A sandwich?'

'Urgh, no. But, I mean, thanks.'

There's a tinkle as someone leaves the café, and it sounds like Miss Annabel peeing.

'So, your school's closed.'

'Yep.'

Some colour arrives in Teddy's cheeks as if he's a Gala apple being polished, hard, on somebody's pullover. He bites his lip. 'You shouldn't go to that school. No one's heard of it. Why don't you go somewhere better? It doesn't even have an entrance exam. Are you stupid?'

'No, I'm not stupid. Well, I don't think so. Anyway, didn't your father arrange it?'

'My father?'

'He's a lawyer, right? Works for my father?'

Teddy glances out of the window and then pauses, as if he has noticed something being killed. 'For now,' he says, frowning. He sips his espresso. Looks down at Natasha's wrist. 'Why are you wearing that during the day?' he says. 'Is it insured? I'm assuming it's real.'

Tash looks down at her bracelet. 'Yeah, it's real,' she says.

'I mean, it's got to be worth a fortune. Please tell me you didn't wear it on the Tube. It's actual diamonds, right?'

Tash shrugs. She's actually worn it every day since her

154

father gave it to her. Even though she knows he didn't choose it, she pretends to herself that he did. Then again, it's not impossible. It's not Aunt Sonja's taste at all. Maybe someone showed him how to go on Net-a-Porter and he went to the jewellery section and chose something and clicked Add to Basket. But it's more likely someone did all that for him. Perhaps even someone like Teddy's father.

'Please tell me you didn't wear it for me.'

'No, I didn't wear it for you.'

They sit in silence for a few seconds as the sun moves behind a cloud and the fluorescence tickles the gravestones.

'Do you want to come to a party?' Tash asks. 'It's in the middle of nowhere, near Cambridge. My friend's sister is getting engaged.'

'Who's your friend?'

'Melissa Porter. Lissa. Her sister's called Susan, I think. Suze.'

'Never heard of them.' He sighs. 'Maybe. It depends what the driver's doing that night. Do you want to come to a ball with me in London?'

'A ball?'

'Yes, a ball. Why do you say it like that?'

Tash laughs. 'Sounds like something from the past. From Tolstoy.'

'Well, here in the UK all the best people still go to them,' he says.

'OK. Um . . . By the way, do you know a boy called Caleb Downlowe?'

155

'Er . . .'

'In Year 11?'

'We don't have that. Do you mean fifth form?'

'I suppose so. He'd be like sixteen. Just sixteen.'

'Is he really pale?'

'Yeah.'

'Father's in banking? Lives in the Middle East some-where?'

'I don't know.'

'Sister who killed herself?'

'Yes! Except she didn't. I mean, I don't think she did.'

'What are you, some kind of Russian Miss Marple?'

'Er, I don't know what that is, so maybe?'

Teddy looks at his watch. 'You can walk back with me if you like,' he says. 'If he's not in class he's probably jerking off one of the other fifth-formers, but we'll knock first.' He looks into her eyes and then down to her breasts. 'Have you ever seen a boy jerk another boy off?'

Tash shakes her head. 'No. Have you?'

'We used to do it all the time in Shell,' he says. 'It's disgusting.'

'Shell?'

'Year 9.' He sighs.

Caleb isn't there, so Tash leaves him a note.

Later, when she tells Aunt Sonja that she went for coffee with Teddy, Aunt Sonja looks amused.

'But what about George?' she says, with a raised eyebrow.

156

'Who's George?'

'The boy at the castle you were supposed to meet.'

Teddy's friend. The one with all the freckles, who left the drawing room with three prostitutes, and his top lip covered with white powder. The one who called Natasha Teddy's 'mail-order bride'. But did he actually say that? Did he specify? Maybe he meant that she was *his* mail-order bride.

'Oh.'

'Nice boy, though, Teddy,' says Aunt Sonja. 'He has no idea what his father really does, of course.'

'What does George's father do?'

'Rapes and pillages and acquires all the spoils of the world.'

'Oh. Great.'

'Right, fuck all this,' says Aunt Sonja, after they've finished their poached fish and quinoa. 'Let's go out and get cocktails and buy opera tickets for the weekend.'

'OK,' says Tash.

They walk across the bridge and the sparkle is overwhelming, just for a second, as an unseen shoal of fish continues darkly towards the estuary and Natasha realises she is never going to marry anyone.

*

The next morning there's a message on Tash's phone. It's from Caleb.

157

What do you want?

Tash sleepily types her reply.

I want to find out what happened to Bianca.

She died.

I know. I'm really sorry. She was my friend.

She was my sister.

Your twin, right?

Right. She killed herself.

I'm not sure that's true.

A long pause, with the app assuring Tash that Caleb is 'typing'.

Me neither. Like I said in the slam book.

OK but someone has Tippexed out what you wrote, so.

Who?

IDK. What did you write?

Not sure. Probably that her school killed her. Because it did.

Will you meet me?

Where?

The French House in Soho?

When?

Whenever suits you.

The French House is where Aunt Sonja took Tash after they'd bought their opera tickets. They'd walked slowly through the back streets of Covent Garden, past bookshops and apothecaries and homeopaths, then crossed Charing Cross Road and entered Chinatown, with its upside-down red chickens and Lucky Cat shops, and then crossed Shaftesbury Avenue to Soho. 'Full of tourists now,' Aunt Sonja had said. 'With their vile factory-made clothes and those stupid rucksacks the wrong way around.' She'd shrugged. 'But I still love it. When I first came to London . . .' She smiled. 'But Soho was different then. It had real sex clubs and beautiful strangers from all over the world, and everyone was poor in money but rich in everything else. Now it is the other way around.'

'Were you poor then?' asked Natasha.

'Oh yes,' said Aunt Sonja. She laughed hollowly. 'You have no idea.'

'How did you get rich?'

'It's complicated,' said Aunt Sonja. 'It started with the usual stuff. Smuggling, prostitution – just in a minor way. And then, well, I'll show you later this week if you like. You can come to my offices.' She winks. 'If you're good.'

They sat at wooden tables drinking Americanos ('Not too alcoholic,' Aunt Sonja had assured Tash, 'only Campari and vermouth. You can have *one*.'). Natasha watched the people coming and going, but tourists are always boring to observe because they always do the same things. Instead Tash started looking at the paintings and photographs on the walls of the French House. One black and white photograph showed a wrinkled, wise, ravaged-looking androgynous woman lying on a patterned carpet holding a burning cigarette. She looked intellectual, free. Her face was un-made-up, but deep. And then on the wall above that, a painting of two

159

women at a table drinking rust-coloured cocktails and laughing together. They seemed so very happy. Natasha could not stop looking at this particular image. It was almost an exact picture of her and Aunt Sonja, even where they were placed at their table, except that in the image Aunt Sonja was much fatter and blonder and wearing glasses. Natasha's hair was darker, and it wasn't actually clear whether she was thin or fat or somewhere in between.

Is it true that sometimes in life you are offered a picture of your future? That you are shown it explicitly, deliberately, in a painting, or as a glimpse of someone walking down a road? Natasha had experienced this only once before in her life, when she was leaving home for Moscow on the bus that would take her almost all the way to the airport. As the bus shuddered out of town Tash looked through the smeared window and saw a skeletony figure in a long dark coat hunched over a twin-buggy that she was pushing into the harsh wind. The woman's face was pinched and grey, and for no reason into Natasha's mind came the thought, 'That's me if I stay here. That's me in an alternative future.' And she felt glad, for the first time, to be leaving.

On the way home they walked through Soho a different way, past a cake shop.

'Look,' said Aunt Sonja. In the window was a red cake in the shape of a heart, and on it, in white icing, the words *I am divorcing you*. She smiled. 'I love it here.'

Today it's warm, and the tourists are all in cheap t-shirts. When Caleb arrives he looks so underage that they have to walk all the way down Dean Street to the Soho Hotel instead. Natasha really wants Cointreau, but as it's only 4 p.m. she settles for Oolong tea, which she pays for on her black Amex, along with a Rooibos for Caleb. All the oos. Caleb really is astonishingly pale and tiny, like those mice that Miss White keeps in a cage for the Year 12s to experiment on. His eyes aren't quite as red, though. Almost, but not quite.

'I'm not sure I can do this,' Caleb says. He's wearing a denim jacket similar to the ones the boys at home wear. Natasha has no idea how it would be possible to obtain a garment like this in London. It's awful. And he must be very warm.

Tash hasn't planned what to say, and when the words come out, they aren't quite what she expected.

'Why couldn't any of us come to the funeral?' she asks.

'That school fucking killed her.'

Natasha bites her lip. Tastes blood. Stops.

'Not her friends. We tried to help her. Or we would have done if we'd known . . .'

He shrugs. Doesn't take off his jacket. Looks like he might cry.

'It wasn't exactly a secret,' he says, 'what was wrong with her.'

Now he does take off his jacket. He folds it up and puts it on the chair. His arms look wrong in some way

161

Tash can't figure out. They are absurdly thin and white with silvery lines on them like tiny snail-trails.

'No,' says Tash. 'I know. I'm sorry.' She pulls up her bag from the floor and puts it next to her on the large sofa. 'It was so weird when we got the slam book back,' Tash says. 'When we opened it, your bit was covered in Tippex, look.' She removes it from her bag, and he snatches it from her as if it is a precious journal he's misplaced. The way he's clutching it makes it seem unlikely that Tash will ever get it back, which would be unfortunate as it belongs to the whole form.

'You have it,' he breathes. 'Thank God.'

'Er . . .'

'I never even took a picture,' he says.

'A picture of what?' says Tash, but he's already flicking to the early section of the book that the girls filled in. And there is the whole page created by Bianca. Beyond noticing the photo Bianca was putting in, Tash hasn't ever looked at this page. Why would she? It was the boys' pages that everyone wanted to see. Everyone wanted to know which girl each boy had picked as his 'fantasy date' (Zoe, Tash and Tiffanie came out well in this, and not one single boy chose Becky with the bad hair), and how the boys had ranked the girls in order (again, Tiffanie, Tash, Zoe as 1, 2 and 3). It didn't occur to anyone to read each other's pages, which actually seems absurd now, because they have certainly missed at least one more chance to laugh at Becky with the bad hair, and find

162

new ways to copy Tiffanie. But then Mr Hendrix was in quite a hurry to take the book and send it off and—

Tash leans over Caleb and regards Bianca's page for the first time. As she does, her bare arm touches his, and he shrinks away. There's a strange watercolour of the lake – like, when exactly did she have a chance to do that? – and on the surface of the lake is a floating corpse with pale physalis hair – obviously Princess Augusta – and in her hands is not the dead flower that she holds in the painting that Bianca has copied, but instead a black, shiny jewel.

'She talked about this in family therapy,' said Caleb.

'About what?'

'About a dead princess floating in a lake. And a black diamond. She made up all this stuff, like—'

'You know that some of it's true, though?' says Tash. She points at the picture. 'I mean, this is Princess Augusta, the founder of our school. And this jewel was apparently given to her by some sultan who—'

'Who raped her and—'

'Ravaged. We prefer *ravaged* to be honest, it's kind of sexier?'

Caleb shoots Tash a dark, perplexed look as if she herself is part of Bianca's demented watercolour of a reality that does not exist, and never did. His blond hair flops into his face and he flicks it away with his hand. He has the cheekbones of the rich, but the eyes of the poor.

163

'And more amusing,' adds Tash. She pours more tea.

'Oh, God,' says Caleb. He goes pale, stands up. 'Look, I just need to . . .'

He leaves his jacket behind. He's gone in the direction of the loos. But how long does it take for a teenage boy to wee? He's gone one minute, then two, then five. Tash thinks again about ordering Cointreau. She frowns, then smiles, then frowns. There's a big mirror here which might be good for a selfie but maybe this is not the time. Is he doing a big poo? Is he crying? Then he's back, with redder eyes and, Tash realises for the first time, crimson, raw hands. The hands are still damp. They flake with bits of bloodied skin. He sits down.

'Are you . . . ?' Begins Natasha. She wants to ask if he's OK, but suddenly the word seems too small and her voice sounds ohso loud and . . .

A clock ticks on the wall. Is he going to leave? Perhaps. He picks up his jacket and unfolds it. But no. In fact he's looking for something in the pockets. An inhaler. He puffs on it, puts it back. Puts his jacket back. Folded.

'Do you know where the diamond came from?' asks Caleb. He asks the way a bored teacher might. A bored teacher in a hot room when everyone is almost asleep. A bored teacher who knows that they will always know more than you, but that this knowledge will always be boring. Although in this case, of course, it's not.

Tash frowns. 'Is it real?'

'Yes.'

'And?'

'It came from India, apparently. Stolen from a temple by some soldier who sold it to some early oligarch who—'

'Oligarch? But—'

'There were oligarchs in the past.'

'Right.'

'The sultan – who was probably not a sultan at all, according to Google – apparently gave Princess Augusta the diamond in return for her purity. And then, according to Bianca, she cast it off in despair, and that's how it ended up at the bottom of a lake in a minor girls' independent school in Hertfordshire.'

'Wait. You're saying the diamond is in the *lake*?'

'I'm saying none of it is true.'

'But it's what Bianca thought?'

'I don't know. You go to that dreadful school. What do you think?' Caleb doesn't wait for an answer. 'Anyway, she said that if she could touch the black diamond she'd get better. She even asked our father for money to dredge the lake, like he was ever going to spend money on something like that.'

'OK, so the black diamond is supposedly at the bottom of our lake. Then . . . Wait, are you saying she went in to get it? That's how she drowned?'

'I don't know. But it's what it says on her death certificate. *Misadventure*. Better than anorexia, don't you think?'

'Um . . . OK, so you originally said that Bianca made all this up, but then you just said you googled it. So is it true or not? Like, does the black diamond actually exist?'

'Oh, the black diamond exists all right,' says Caleb. 'Or at least *a* black diamond from India with a curse. It's just not at the bottom of your school lake.'

'How do you know?'

'Because it's in the Smithsonian.'

*

'Can I get a lift with you to the gym?' Rachel asks her brother.

'Are you sure you want to go?' says their mother. 'I'm not sure you'll be able to do anything with that arm.'

'Well,' says Elliot. 'I'm leaving now this second, so.'

'OK, I'm coming,' says Rachel. It's taken her hours this morning to get ready. Dressing with one arm is no fun. But she's going to see Jordon for the first time since the last Exeat, when he actually asked her if she'd go out with him sometime. She gave him her number then but he hasn't messaged her yet. Of course, he did say he's not good with words, so maybe she shouldn't have expected anything. And no one from his world really understands about boarding school. Anyway, she's here now. And there are weeks ahead when she can . . . What? What exercise can she actually do with a broken arm? This is what she's hoping someone at the gym will tell her, because she has no clue. She can't run: she's

166

already tried that. She's still doing a hundred sit-ups a day, but . . .

Something's going wrong.

Rachel blames Matron, she really does, because ever since she had that conversation with her, all she's done is put on weight. The first four pounds arrived literally overnight. Yes, on the Monday when she got home Rachel went to bed weighing one thing and then when she got up she was four fucking pounds heavier. So, OK, fluctuations, and water retention and all that blahblah. Fine. But it's now a week later and all that's happened is she has put on *another* two pounds. But how? Why? It's actually showing too, in a little roll of fat around her middle. So she's wearing an old baggy vest of her mother's rather than the crop top she'd planned for this encounter. She still hasn't had her navel pierced. Something odd has happened to her hair too. She looks fucking terrible.

'Come on, if you're coming,' says Elliot.

He's lost interest in her. He's changed recently in other ways too: for example, he's given up veganism and now only eats meat. He even, the previous night, ate a meat sandwich, where the 'bread' was just more meat. Chicken in beef. Rachel had one too, because it wasn't that many calories, and she needs her protein, because protein builds muscle and muscle burns fat. Elliot and Jordon now spend much of their free time in the CrossFit gym, which is more real and serious and authentic than the lame-ass

167

municipal place where Jordon still works. In fact, Elliot is only going there now to drop off a mysterious package that he makes Rachel hold in her lap while he drives there.

'What even is this?' she asks.

'Protein powder,' he says. 'Juice. Nothing you need to worry about.'

Rachel's missed the smell of the gym, the sweet herbal aroma of boy hormones mixed with the heady perfume of sweaty, hard-worn plastic. Jordon looks way more muscular than she remembers. And indeed, his name tops the 'bicep circumference' leader-board on the wall by the Smith machine. Elliot's name isn't there, but then Elliot probably doesn't care any more, now that he does CrossFit.

Jordon is busy, and so doesn't notice Rachel at first. He's got a clipboard, and he's encouraging an attractive young woman on the rowing machine. Obviously one of his clients, or someone being given a gym induction. The twins, Millie and Izzy, wave to her from the office, but then one says something to the other and they giggle silently behind the glass. Was that in fact a *sarcastic* wave? But why? Elliot has disappeared into the back of the office, where he's talking to the boxing instructor, Hard Mike. Hard Mike is at least fifty, but only has 5 per cent body fat. He wears khaki all the time, runs bootcamps on a Sunday in the park and lives entirely on pork and frozen peas.

The woman gets off the rowing machine. She has the exact body Rachel wants. She's tall, but not too tall, and lean. Her booty is plump, but not too plump. She has breasts rather like Tiffanie's. She's wearing black shorts – shorts! – and a sheer Nike vest top. Now Jordon gets on the rowing machine and she's shouting instructions at him, and he's doing what she tells him, and then at one point she's shouting out his current time and he's sweating and looking in her eyes and grinning, but the way a wolf would grin, and the twins come out and one of them says to Rachel, 'That's Heidi. She's the new PT.'

'Oh,' is all Rachel can say. Jordon still does not notice her. Now he and Heidi move on to the mats, and it's like they're having some sort of competition – perhaps that's what the clipboard is for – and now they're doing that thing where you take one of those big Swiss balls and lie down with it behind your head and then sit up and put it between your feet and then lie flat again and then pass the ball back to your hands and so on. Jordon makes a joke and Heidi throws the Swiss ball at him and now it's his turn. They look happy, so happy. Rachel wants to be sick. Heidi is a vision of what she wanted to be, but now someone else has got there first, and in an instant Rachel doesn't want it any more.

'She can actually beat him on the rowing challenge,' says Millie admiringly.

'Have you done the rowing challenge yet?' Izzy asks Rachel.

169

Rachel points to her broken arm. 'Can't really row,' she says.

'Oh yeah. Meant to say, sorry about that,' says Izzy. She makes a sympathetic face that seems a bit sarcastic, like the wave.

Elliot comes out of the office. Hard Mike is now stuffing the package Elliot gave him into the bottom of his sports bag.

'Right,' Elliot says. 'How much longer are you going to be?'

Rachel shrugs. 'I don't know,' she says. 'I'm not sure what I can do with my arm like this.'

'Maybe Jordon will have some ideas,' says Elliot. 'Hey, man.'

Jordon has come over. 'Hey, bro,' he says to Elliot, slapping his back.

'It's all in there with Hard Mike,' says Elliot.

'Thanks, man.'

'Hi, Jordon,' says Rachel.

'Oh, hi,' he says. He shakes his head as if he's got water in his ears; in fact, as if the water in his ears has made him temporarily forget who Rachel is, but now, after a few more shakes, he remembers. 'How's it going?'

'Good, thanks. You?'

Heidi walks past and makes her fingers into the shape of a T and raises her dark arched eyebrows. Jordon grins at her and nods.

'Nice to see you,' says Jordon, to Rachel. He turns

towards the office, then stops, then turns back. 'Actually,' he says, 'I wanted to ask you something.'

Rachel's legs. Her heart. The world tilts. 'Yes?'

He moves a few feet away to stand nearer to the wall, and she follows. He stands close to her now, as if what he's asking is a secret. Not secret enough to go into the office, but still something special just between them. She can smell his deodorant, which thankfully doesn't completely cover that deep sweet testosterone smell she would do anything for. She'd bathe in it, if she could. Drown in it. He grins, although it's a kind of fake grin. It's a fake grin that says *Don't hate me for what I'm about to say.*

'So I'm doing case studies for my PT training and I'm looking for volunteers who won't mind spending a bit of time with me, you know, being my guinea pig?' He grins again. 'So I need someone really athletic, and someone who's like a fitness beginner, who's maybe like a bit fat and just starting to get into shape?' He looks Rachel up and down. 'So Heidi's going to be my athletic case study. Will you be my beginner?'

There is a moment for this to travel through Rachel's ears and into her brain, where it is briefly processed and—

'Are you fucking serious?' says Rachel, backing away.

'Rachel!' says Elliot. 'Settle down. Sorry,' he adds, to Jordon.

'Don't be offended,' says Jordon to Rachel. 'I mean,

171

you've been training for less than a year. And I mean, compared with Heidi . . .'

'Fuck this,' says Rachel to Elliot. 'Let's go. Let's get out of this pathetic, windowless, dirty, small-town excuse for a gym, full of people who are *extremely* up themselves given that they are basically just cleaners with clipboards and absolutely no future.' She has the lungs for this kind of sentence now, because she is not a fucking beginner. She looks at Jordon. 'You think you're so fucking important, because your arms are bigger than some other guy's? But you don't actually have a brain, so why would you matter to anybody? Have you ever read a book? No. All you are is flesh and muscle, like a farm animal. You're basically livestock. You've devoted your life to being artificially bulked up, like a fucking cow, like a sodding battery hen. And you know what's really sad? You could have chosen *anything*, and you chose that, to be like all the rest of the pathetic cattle.' She leaves without saying goodbye to the twins, or Hard Mike, all of whom watch her go but don't say anything. She stands sobbing by the car until Elliot gets there. What's he been doing all his time? Probably apologising for her, his stuck-up fat sister.

'Why were you such a bitch to Jordon?' he says, once they are in the car. He seems genuinely surprised by Rachel, who never usually surprises anyone.

'Because he's a fucking cunt,' says Rachel, through her tears.

'And I mean, the gym? You can't go back there now.'

'I don't fucking want to.'

After that, the weight keeps on coming. A pound a day for seven days. Rachel's been eating 1500 calories a day, but now takes this down to 1000. The weight gain stops for a few days, and then resumes, with a cosmic flourish and a big *Haha!* and a bout of embarrassing flatulence. Rachel sobs as she stands on the scales in her en-suite bathroom, the week before school starts again. Do tears weigh something? Maybe she can cry it all out. She howls at the sky, at God, at Heidi and every other woman like her.

'What the fuck do you want from me?' she screams at the universe.

'I want your blood,' the universe says back. 'All of it. I'm going to punish you for being such a stuck-up snob, and for what you said to Jordon.'

Or is that just her imagination? Is that something the universe would actually say? Maybe. Wasn't the universe a bit mean and shouty in that Keats poem the headmaster read to them that time?

On the kitchen table there's a book called *The Fast Diet*. It's got a bookshop sticker on it that makes it look as though its actual title is *The Fast Die*. Rachel's mother must have bought it. Rachel gets a glass of water and takes the book up to her bedroom. Fasting. Right. Blahblahblahblah. It's spiritual. Blahblahblahblah. It helps you lose weight.

173

So what actually *is* fasting in this book? OK. It's 500 calories a day.

Rachel googles this, because it's quicker than reading any more of the book.

500 calories a day. Wasn't that what Anastasia said actually worked? Rachel is clearly one of those people who is so sensitive to food that she needs to go that low. Well, she can. She can do it. And she does. And then, only then, does the weight start to shift again, to declare itself beaten and slink off back to wherever it came from, or at least to wait in a dark, cobwebby corner for Rachel to fail again, when it will return to punish her, worse each time, just like Matron said.

*

The dining table in the flat is beautifully laid for two, with silver cutlery and white linen napkins. On the kitchen counter is a large white iced cake, a fresh rye loaf, a half-bottle of dark dessert wine and a receipt for some black truffles. The truffles are sitting like shrivelled little kings in the fridge. Keeping them company is a bottle of Bollinger and a complex cheese-board.

'I have changed my views on food,' says Aunt Sonja, when Natasha comes out of the shower and visibly starts when she sees the cake. The last time sugar was in this flat may have even been before Aunt Sonja moved in. Wait – didn't she have some pink-champagne chocolates once? Maybe. Had someone sent them to her? Tash vaguely remembers finding one spat out and leaking through a crumpled tissue in the kitchen bin and then Aunt Sonja saying something about having given them to a homeless man on the Embankment.

'Tonight, we eat,' she says. 'We eat whatever we want. And you tell me about your investigation. And then tomorrow I'm going to take you to my office and show you what I do.'

'OK.'

'What do you want? I was craving truffles, champagne and cake, but there's also celeriac remoulade and pâté in the fridge. I also managed to get hold of a black watermelon. If you want anything else we can send out for it.'

'No, that sounds lovely,' says Tash. 'But . . .'

Aunt Sonja is going to the fridge for the champagne. She pops the cork and then pours two glasses.

'You are old enough for a couple of glasses of champagne, right?'

'Oh yes,' says Tash.

She actually turned sixteen a few days before and wondered if anyone would notice, but they didn't. Not old enough for champagne; well, not legally, but old enough to go to Selfridges with her black Amex and buy a pair of pointed cowboy boots with gold buckles. Frustratingly, these have not satisfied her in the way she'd thought they would. Whenever she puts them on all she thinks of is Nico and how impressed he'd be to see her wearing them, and how much more that makes her hate him.

They sit on the sofa with the champagne. Aunt Sonja has poured it into the best crystal saucers, rather than the usual flutes. She presses a button and jazz starts playing through the hidden speaker system in the flat.

'Right. I'm going to show you some pictures,' says Aunt Sonja. She gets her phone. Presses a few more buttons. 'You're going to tell me what they have in common.'

Natasha is still looking at the phone until she realises that the pictures are also on the television screen. Now she looks up. Here, one by one, are all the powerful women of the world. Angela Merkel, Hillary Clinton, Theresa May, Oprah Winfrey. Then come some that Natasha doesn't recognise, but have the same aura. They seem to all be in the throes of a television interview or giving speeches on stages, wearing Madonna mics and shiny patent beige stilettoes and—

'What do they have in common?' asks Aunt Sonja.

'I was going to say that they're all fat, but these ones aren't fat,' says Tash.

Indeed, the one on screen at the moment is a youngish dark-haired woman in a red satin dress with perfect arms that Bianca would have said were fat, probably, but are not. They are the colour of piano keys and so long and toned and—

176

'Well, this one's obviously been airbrushed,' says Aunt Sonja. She sips her champagne. 'But try harder. What do they have in common?'

Tash shrugs. 'They're all powerful?'

'Yes, and?'

'Um, maybe rich?'

'Yes, they are all richer than your father, in fact. Many of them are billionaires. Do you know what that means?'

'I guess, having more than a billion pounds?'

'Dollars, actually. But what does it *mean*?'

'I don't know. Um, you can do what you want?'

'Well, sort of. Actually, some of these women can't do exactly what they want, at least not in public, because they run companies and countries and people expect certain things from them. They're role models, which can be constraining. Come on. What do they look like to you?'

'God, I don't know. All different. Not that attractive necessarily. I mean, only one of them is really skinny, and she's got massive glasses and weird hair and . . .'

'"All different",' repeats Aunt Sonja. 'Good. OK. Now look at these pictures.'

She presses a few more buttons, and up come the celebrities, women famous for acting and singing and dancing and charming and entertaining. They all look, they all look . . .

'These ones all look the same,' says Natasha.

'This is what I have discovered,' says Aunt Sonja. 'This

is one of the puzzles of being a woman. This is what you have to think about as you grow up. How powerful do you think these same-looking celebrities actually are?'

Natasha's heart suddenly fills with love for Aunt Sonja, who, she now realises, is trying to give her some moral instruction, some basic feminist grounding. Aunt Sonja, with her skinny arms and sad eyes and bad relationships, who lives all alone in this soulless rich person's apartment, who has a cleaner and a PA and business of her own but who is clearly so very unhappy, Aunt Sonja actually loves Natasha, and that is why she is doing this. Tash's eyes fill with tears.

'It's OK,' says Tash. 'Thank you. I mean, I see what you're saying, and it's reallyreally interesting, and soso right, but, you know, I'm not anorexic. You don't need to worry about me in that way. Some girls at school obviously are, and, like, it's got really out of hand lately, but it's just not me. I even tried to catch anorexia because I wanted to be thin – basically to look like those people on screen – I mean the celebrities – but I couldn't. I'm not going to lie. I did try. But my brain just isn't wired that way.'

'OK,' says Aunt Sonja. 'Good. I can see that. But mine is.'

'But—'

'Don't be like me.'

They eat hot pasta with truffle grated over it, then pâté and salad, then the cheese and the cake. Tash feels oddly steadied by the food she has eaten: like a ship that has just come through a storm. Aunt Sonja switches off the television and asks Tash all about her meeting with Caleb, and nods and frowns and then talks about blockchain until it's time for bed. As Tash goes to sleep she can hear the familiar sound of Aunt Sonja vomiting in her bathroom, but this time maybe a bit less than usual. And all the images of women she's seen disappear from her mind, and she is left with only one picture: the woman with the cigarette in the black and white photograph from the wall of the French House.

*

Everything smells of cheap paint. Miss Annabel can't stand it. Cheap paint, bleach, the fags of the contract cleaners. The vomit smell still lingers on the first floor, despite all of the attention it's been paid. She shudders. Slips a little on the grand staircase, because the backward women from the village didn't understand that you don't use polish to clean wooden stairs because it's dangerous. Someone should warn the girls? Or maybe not.

Anyway, now some bruises on her shins to go with the ones all over her arms that she has hidden today with a lemon cardigan. Tomorrow, the same one in shell pink, then back to the lemon again. Her Achilles tendon doesn't feel quite right. Her lungs ache. When are the girls coming back? Without the girls, this hollow old building has no meaning at all. With them it's almost as bad, but at least the time passes more quickly. The sound of their pointless activities is at least a barrier between this world in which Miss Annabel finds herself, and the blindfold nothingness beyond.

*

The message subject is *Legal Action to be brought by Captain Downlowe.* Is he a captain? Who cares? It sounds better. It sounds like something from the BBC period dramas that Aunt Sonja enjoys on a Sunday evening. Tash has taken to this remarkably easily. It didn't take long, during Tash's first visit to Aunt Sonja's offices, for her to learn how to send a phishing email for someone's passwords. So now she's practising on the headmaster, because why wouldn't you? And also because she actually wants the headmaster's passwords because she wants to know everything he knows. Or, at least, everything in his emails.

The morning after the champagne and the feminism Natasha found a USB drive on the floor in the kitchen, which had the word SECRET written on it in silver Sharpie. She put the kettle on and regarded the plastic device for a few seconds before putting it on top of Aunt Sonja's things on the counter: her diary and her phone and her iPad. She must have dropped it. Or, actually, that silver Sharpie detail was a bit obvious, so . . .

'Well done,' said Aunt Sonja, as they got into the car

to be taken to the office in Bloomsbury. 'You've passed the test.'

'Test? Oh. The USB?' said Natasha.

'Do you know how many people would have taken that and put it in their computer?'

Tash shook her head.

'Almost everyone. But you're clever. And trustworthy.'

For the rest of the week, Natasha had learned all about what happens to the people who put those USBs in their computers. Sometimes all their files are wiped out, just like that, to teach them a lesson. But more often it just allows the gentle insertion of a little file with the instruction to send copies of everything to the original owner of the USB, who is usually Aunt Sonja or one of her colleagues.

The headmaster opens the document. Of course he does. Tash gets the subtle vibration that says her virus is in his computer in the last five minutes of prep, when Sin-Jin is asleep and snoring even though it's still light and summery outside. When the bell goes, the girls simply leave her sitting there in her chair, head drooped like an old, dead swan.

Rachel has swapped with Dani, so now she has Bianca's old bed. Dani was having nightmares in it, but Rachel – so much thinner now after the break – said she enjoyed nightmares. 'I like them really dark and violent,' she said, with no expression on her pale face.

'Well, er, good,' said Dani. 'Enjoy.'

181

Has anyone changed those sheets yet? Nope. Someone's painted the walls, though.

Rachel doesn't go for runs any more. She sits on her bed with her headphones in looking at pictures on her phone and listening to *Abbey Road*. She doesn't sell her clean-eating guides to the crushlets now. Madame Vincent sends an email to the headmaster, registering her concern. Then the headmaster emails Rachel and asks her to go and see him at his house if she has any troubles she wants to share with him, anything at all. Maybe she will; maybe she won't. It all depends how she feels.

Mrs Cuckoo is retiring and so the Year 11 girls are given the task of helping to organise all the many cook-books she's accumulated in the school kitchen. It's supposed to help with the stress of revising for the upcoming exams. Someone has had the idea that a section should be created in the school library for these books, most of which still include margarine in cake recipes, and one of which actually has recipes for curried hare.

'Oh my God,' says Rachel, when the girls open the book onto the full-page picture of the hare, its skinned pink and grey body laid out with all its legs splayed like extreme, bad-taste pornography. 'I'm going to be—'

But then Rachel is always looking for excuses these days: excuses to throw up, or pass out, or take to her bed. She has migraines, stomach-ache, leg-ache, arm-ache, temporary blindness. She shivers all the time. She is growing hair in improbable places. The moustache hasn't come back, but instead she has this fine downy fluff all over her face, as if she's a polar bear cub, or a pale shrew. But somehow she is also becoming more and more beautiful. No one wants to admit it, because it is so fucked up, but there is something truly compelling in her frail boniness. It's not so great when she's naked, that's true: but in clothes she looks the fucking bomb.

Maybe that's why no one does anything.

Dominic and Tony are still haunting the school. They have a 'clinic' on a Friday when girls can go to them with their 'issues'. The crushlets go and moan about home-sickness and mild bullying, and the Year 10s go to talk about their career options. One of the Year 9s has actually managed to develop a crush on Tony and goes there with her skirt rolled up about as far as it will go to discuss when he thinks she should lose her virginity and how. Natasha hates Dominic and Tony so much that she goes nowhere near the Dower House on a Friday. She doesn't ever want to see Dominic again, or have to deal with any more of his thoughts on *abuse*. So between French and history she now walks the long way around, past the sheep chomping on the dry grass, then down by the lake.

There *is* a sparkle. For real. A sort of black glint, right in the middle of the water. She can definitely see it now.

And, in an upstairs room in the headmaster's house, a familiar thin silhouette looking out across the surface of the dark deep. A roman nose in profile. Rachel. She is macilent, yes, but magnificent too, under his instruction. But the real question is this: is she a good enough swimmer?

*

No one particularly wants to get expelled so close to exams, or indeed Suze's party. Everyone knows that parents are funny about troublemakers. But still.

'We'll sign out in the Walks book after lunch,' says Tash. 'Nip to Stevenage and be back in time for supper. Literally no one will know.'

'I am certainement go-*ange*,' says Tiffanie. She's back to her normal self now, after going home for Easter. Her extra fat has gone. Is she still 'skinny fat'? Probably, but she doesn't care. As long as she looks OK on the outside, which she does, why should she care? Like, pretty much every single boy in fifth form at Harrow seemed to think she was the most attractive girl in the school, so. And she's rich, and French.

'I mean, I really don't *need* anyone else to come,' says Tash. 'But . . .'

But Donya is definitely coming. And Dani. Everyone wants to see Mr Hendrix again, to have another stab at getting him to fall in love with them, or at least show them one of his tattoos. And of course everyone wants to see what Tash is up to, because she's not really saying anything. The only thing they have to do is agree not to tell Rachel.

Or Lissa, because Lissa will probably tell Rachel if she knows. And Lissa can't be compromised because of the party. Being banned from going to a party is something that can be worked around. But if the party was cancelled altogether? Or if Lissa's friends were uninvited? No.

What's the worst that can happen? The rest of the form is sworn to secrecy via Ayesha, who catches the apples approaching the school gates in jeans and does not believe the walk story, not for a minute. But Tash doesn't say where they're really off to: she says they're going to London in secret so Tiffanie can sleep with one of the Harrow boys. Big mistake. You could normally rely on Sin-Jin and Madame Vincent and Miss Annabel to go through a whole Sunday without noticing that four of the most troublesome girls in the school are missing. Madame Vincent has a new catalogue full of things you can dress poodles in. And half a bottle of sherry. And a letter from her sister in Paris. Sin-Jin has a box of rose and violet creams and a violent American novel. Miss Annabel has her bruises, and a whole crushlet ballet to choreograph. But no sixteen-year-old can keep a secret for longer than half an hour and so they go to the head-master's office, sob-wracked, to confess on the apples' behalf. It's Becky with the bad hair, of course. It always bloody well is. With Bella and Elle in tow. And Ayesha, saying she really didn't mean to get anyone in trouble.

*

Mr Hendrix is not pleased to see them. Not at all.

'Where the hell did you get this address?' he asks.

His flat is on one of the melancholy pedestrianised streets where everything is shut because it's Sunday. It's above a charity shop that has a summer-themed window with slink mannequins from the olden days in summer dresses with high heels. The dresses have been belted in a way you would rarely belt a dress in normal life, but it doesn't really matter on this witnessless street that looks like it's been prepped for a zombie apocalypse.

Tash doesn't say that in fact she's now got everything she could ever want to know about Mr Hendrix: his date of birth and all his passwords and his bank account details and how veryvery overdrawn he is and all the books he buys from Amazon despite being an anti-capitalist. At least the books themselves are anti-capitalist. Well, sort of. They are all paperbacks by men on atheism and war and the crumbling health service and awful things that happen in Africa. He is a member of an online dating service. Mr Hendrix! With his beautiful eyes and his lovely thick hair. It is this last detail that has made Natasha vow never again to use her new powers in a voyeuristic way. She should have just got his address and left the rest of his hard drive alone. She tries to erase the details from her mind. The receipt for another tattoo; a digital download of the newest, most expensive video-game ever made; a subscription to Apple Music, to a local gym—

186

'Can we come in?' asks Tash.

'No you cannot fucking come in,' he says. 'Jesus.'

He's dressed in gym clothes. He looks a bit sweaty. Is that why?

'Um . . .' Tash takes a step forward. 'But—'

'What are you trying to do? Get me locked up as a sodding paedophile?'

'We're actually all over sixteen now, sir,' says Donya.

He shudders. 'I'm not your teacher any more, thank God. Don't call me "sir".'

'What do your new girls call you?'

'Yeah, what do all the Emilys and Hannahs call you, sir?'

He doesn't reply. But he doesn't shut the door either. From what he's saying, he should be slamming the door in their faces, but he isn't.

'Didn't you like being our teacher?' asks Dani.

'It was a job,' he says. 'But since you've asked, actually no. No, I did not like being your teacher.'

'Why not?' asks Donya.

He sighs. 'That fucking place. And you. You're all so shallow and annoying and . . .' There's a long pause. He clearly thinks one of them is going to interrupt him to defend themselves, but they don't. Instead, Donya's eyes fill with tears. No one says anything, they just regard him sadly.

'And of course in the end you actually managed to kill one of your teachers,' says Mr Hendrix, into the sad

187

silence. 'Bravo. And – guess what? – I had an awful feeling I'd be next. Because you're actually evil. And now you're here. Now you're after me, just as I feared.'

'I thought you didn't believe in evil,' says Tash.

'Is that all you can say?' says Mr Hendrix. 'Is that literally all you can fucking say?'

He looks like he might cry. Teachers are not supposed to cry. But he isn't their teacher any more. He walks into his flat, leaving the door open, so they follow him in. He goes into the small kitchen and opens a cupboard. The girls stand in the front room listening to the creak and bang of cheap plywood and MDF. A stifled sob, and then a slam. No one sits on the drab dark furniture. There's a peace lily in a large pot by the window. It has a single white flower and a lot of brown leaves. On the floor in front of the television is a PlayStation controller and a pile of marking. There's a takeaway pizza box under the coffee table. It's no wonder Mr Hendrix can't get a girlfriend if he lives like this. And also if he goes around calling innocent people murderers and then actually crying.

He comes back from the kitchen with a glass of clear liquid.

'Vodka,' he says. 'Do you want some? Let's all get drunk, and then I can seduce you against your will even though there's four of you, because have you heard that women are now so weak and so pathetic that any man can do whatever he chooses to any of them at any time?

Just because he has a dick! Even if it's small, even if he's impotent, even if he ejaculates prematurely, even if he is so shy he can barely speak to a girl, let alone try to kiss her, let alone . . .' He shuts his eyes. When he opens them again they are shooting death-rays of something that might be fear or sadness or just hatred. 'Just by being here, you could ruin me. You must know that? And you must realise that if I were to even so much as touch one of your skinny arms without asking first then that would pretty much end my life? Even if I asked first, I'd still be in danger. And if I dared to help you when you were drunk? If I dared to help you get into bed so that the other teachers didn't find out and suspend you and—'

'We have kept saying nothing happened with Dr Morgan,' says Tiffanie.

'This was not Natasha and Tiffanie's fault,' says Donya. 'It's true. They always said he was innocent.'

'We didn't even know he was dead until after the Christmas holidays,' says Dani. 'No one ever asked any of us what actually happened.'

'But—'

'We think someone's trying to cover up Bianca's murder,' says Tash. 'And maybe even that Dr Morgan was murdered too.'

'Why are you doing this?' says Mr Hendrix.

'You taught us to question things, sir,' says Dani. 'And now we're questioning them.'

Tash had filled in the others on the train and the walk

189

here. Her suspicions about the headmaster. All the evidence. What Caleb wrote. And who Tippexed it out? Who even *owns* Tippex nowadays? And now Rachel getting thinner and thinner and going to the headmaster's house more and more often, just like Bianca did. Tash has seen her there more than once now. Seen her upstairs. But what are they supposed to do about it? If they say something they'll probably get expelled. But how can they not say something? When Tash told them about the black diamond Tiffanie sort of gasped and said 'Mais non' several times and then it turned out that Bianca had told her all about the black diamond as well. How much she needed it.

'She told me that le diamant noir really exists,' said Tiffanie. 'That if you can hold it you can purify yourself. She said she was learning how to get it.'

'What? How?' said Tash.

'From Dr Moone. He tell her all about it from a book.'

'Oh my God. And now Rachel . . .'

Tash has not told the others that she has hacked the headmaster's computer. That seems déclassé, somehow. Vulgar. And anyway, there wasn't really anything super-interesting on his hard drive. Just some old admin about the business with Dr Morgan. Emails confirming with Amaryllis Archer that the case against him was now closed. Fobbing off the tabloids. The official version for the outside world: both suicides; Bianca because of her anorexia, and Dr Morgan because of general sadness maybe or maybe not related to his desire for young girls. The thing about Dr Morgan and the girls played *down* for the outside world but of course played *up* for the school. But why? The last remaining young male member of staff leaving the school at this difficult time. And the headmaster still there, with his fondness for seeing slender young girls on their own at his house late at night and reading them tenebrous poetry and giving them advice on their beauty.

'We want you to help us,' says Tash to Mr Hendrix.

But he just laughs. He laughs and downs the whole glass of vodka, and then goes and locks himself in his bathroom until they leave.

*

On the train back, Natasha notices that the fields are full of solar panels. One field has also maybe ten sheep, one of which looks dead, and then more solar panels. If you were wild in this landscape, what would you eat, once you'd eaten all the sheep? Humans can't eat grass, or solar panels. It's as if the world is gearing up for a long bout of anorexia, its citizens all big-eyed schoolgirls with their skirts rolled up too short. Can seven billion people live on electricity alone? You can cook all day and all night but there's nothing to cook.

'Do you think Mr Hendrix is right?' says Donya.

'About what?'

'I don't know. All his existentialist anti-capitalist stuff from before.'

'Non,' says Tiffanie. 'He is a fuck-*ange* coward. He is not an existentialist.'

'I don't even know what existentialism is,' says Dani.

'C'est Sartre,' says Tiffanie. 'Et De Beauvoir. Avec les Gauloises á la Rive Gauche. Et Camus, et . . .' She carries on mumbling in French as the guard approaches.

'Right, girls,' he says. 'You do realise you're sitting in first class?'

They look at him blankly.

'Er, yes,' says Tash.

'Can I see your tickets? If they're not first-class you're going to have to move to another carriage and hope that I don't decide to fine you.'

'The ticket office was shut at Stevenage.' Tash hands him her black Amex.

Tiffanie giggles. 'Do you think he has a dib-dob?' she asks.

The guard ignores this. 'You want four first-class singles from Stevenage to . . . ?'

'Hitchin. Thanks.'

'You know these seats are exactly the same as the other ones,' he says.

'Um . . .'

'Come on, girls,' he says. 'Why don't you just move to standard with everyone else? You're getting off in a minute anyway.'

'We want to stay here,' says Tiffanie. 'Do you have a buffet car?' She pauses. 'With dib-dobs?'

'Now, girls, come on,' he says. 'There's no need for this. Don't be silly.' He looks at Natasha's black Amex. 'Is this even a real credit card? I'm not sure you can use these in this country.'

'It's real,' says Tash.

'And you haven't stolen it?'

'Monsieur Dib-dob?' says Tiffanie. 'Are you a secret existentialist?'

He sighs. 'Right, that's it. I've had enough of you. It's a good job you're getting off at the next station or I'd have to throw you off.'

*

Madame Vincent has volunteered to wait by the school gates, not that anyone really needed to. Like, exactly where are the fugitives going to go? They can't stay away forever, and when they get back . . . Well, when they get back, they are instantly suspended anyway. They're sent to their dorms to pack, and they are not allowed to speak to each other, or any of the other girls. They are told that the headmaster is too angry even to see them.

As they walk up the grand staircase Becky with the bad hair is waiting for them.

'Thanks a lot,' she hisses as they go past. 'You do know

you've got the whole form into trouble? They've cancelled the end-of-year disco because of you.'

'You should have kept your mouths shut,' growls Tiffanie.

In Natasha's cubby-hole there is another letter from Nico, which she adds to the others in a pile in her wardrobe. She does not take them with her. Why would she? If she did, she'd have to open them and she can't. And the more of them there are, the more she can't.

Aunt Sonja is in Moscow on business, so Natasha goes to Paris with Tiffanie. It's not much of a punishment, to be honest, spending day after day in Beaubourg cafés and vintage shops and watching *Les Enfants du Paradis* on Tiffanie's large television in her bedroom. They hang out in front of the Pompidou Centre, watching the jugglers and street artists and dreaming, not seriously, of poverty. They watch *Flashdance*. They talk about going clubbing, but in the end they don't have the nerve, and they don't know where to go.

On a mild Saturday morning they take the Eurostar to St Pancras and buy bad coffee from Kings Cross – just like Tash did on her first rainy night in England – and they take the train to Cambridge where they get a taxi to Lissa and Suze's place for the party. Tiffanie and Tash are wearing white silk pussy-bow blouses with ripped 501s and cowboy boots, all from the vintage shops. They've put on a lot of expensive make-up. All these recent days walking around Paris looking at boys, but what are you supposed to say to them? At the party they will at least get to meet some boys properly. Boys that won't be afraid of their diamond earrings, and their sass.

There are only two things bothering Tash. Well, three. She hasn't heard from Aunt Sonja for a few days, which is odd. And at Gare du Nord station her black Amex was rejected. It didn't really matter, as Tiffanie simply put the tickets on her debit card, but Natasha had a horrible feeling that the next time she tried it, it wouldn't work again. Or the time after that. And indeed, it was rejected at Kings Cross, and Tiffanie didn't care; she was happy to pay again because, after all, Natasha has always been so generous with her magic card. But what if the magic has run out? What then? And of course there's Rachel, whom no one has seen or heard from for ages. The suspension was for a week, and now it's Exeat again. She's been at school all that time with only Lissa for company, but Lissa's been so distracted thinking about the party. Anyway, Rachel will be there tonight. Natasha is going to ask her straight out what the headmaster is up to, although she thinks she knows. And then what? What do you do with the truth when you have it? But that's phase two.

There are fairy lights draped around the door and the windows of the cottage. It's possibly a fire hazard with the thatched roof, but Lissa and Suze's mother and step-father are in New York and no one else cares. The conservatory has more fairy lights, and several ice buckets with vodka, gin, tequila and prosecco. No champagne, because Suze and Danny are paying for this themselves, because no one really approves of their engagement. Nothing that stains, because of Danny's teeth. But everyone loves prosecco anyway, and this one was on special offer at Lidl. Suze doesn't mind going in Lidl. Suze doesn't really mind anything, if there's a reason for it.

There's a marquee. Don't even ask who's paying for that, or how fucking difficult it was to put up. And beyond the marquee, the ancient summer house with its peeling green paint and old tattered sofa bed with stained blankets that are more like rugs. Did a dog sleep here once? It is on this sofa bed that Teddy waits for Tash, with a packet of Marlboro and a bottle of Cointreau with two cheap tumblers from the kitchen because he couldn't find any better glasses, and doesn't care any more.

'There's like a guy here asking for you?' says Lissa when Tash arrives. And, OK, yes, this is a bit embarrassing, but also kind of glamorous because Teddy has arrived in a chauffeur-driven car without an invitation but wearing a dinner jacket and black tie with a bottle of 1999 Bollinger as a gift.

'Sit down,' he says to her, when she enters the summer house.

She's holding a flute of prosecco and her face is flushed with the journey from Paris, and the warm evening. Outside, an English bird sings lustily of berries and beauty and bounty and—

'Our fathers are in prison,' Teddy says. 'Here.' He passes her a glass of Cointreau.

'What?' says Natasha. She puts down the prosecco and takes the glass Teddy's offering her instead. She sits next to him.

'Do you want to have sex?' he says. 'I'll probably never see you again after this.'

Tash sips the Cointreau. Lights a Marlboro.

'It's my father's fault that your father's in prison, actually,' Teddy says. 'He made a stupid mistake when he was moving some money around. He was probably drunk. It's dark money, of course. Do you know what that means?'

'Sort of? I read this book, but—'

'They don't cover any of this in Theology and Philosophy at Harrow,' says Teddy. 'Although you'd think they would. It would be bloody useful. What do you do when you find out that your father is so rich because he helps other men – men like your father – hide and spend the money they've made from drugs and prostitutes and sweatshops and fracking and illegal slaughterhouses and pesticides and pollutants and—'

'That's not what my father does.'

'Really?'

'He owns a phone company.'

'Right.' Teddy sips his Cointreau. 'They're going to extradite him. He's going back to Moscow. To prison there. All his assets will be stripped.' He reaches for one

197

of Natasha's breasts and holds onto it, while their breathing becomes audible and ragged. Tash puts down her drink and her cigarette and leans towards Teddy. His pale face. His breath smells of tobacco and orange peel. Their teeth clink as they kiss. His tongue is drier than she thought it would be. Teddy reaches under Natasha's silk shirt and then beneath the stiff wire of her bra and his hand is sweaty but she wants to go with him into oblivion, into whatever this is. To share these last moments of whatever their lives have been. For Natasha this will surely mean going back to Russia, to her mother, to her one stained pillow. What's worse, Teddy's fate, or hers? But Teddy will be all right. He's English, at least. He'll do his A Levels and get a scholarship to Oxford, because his father still knows people, and anyway, he wasn't really to blame. It was all just jolly bad luck and what happens when you get mixed up with the Russians, who—

How to stop these thoughts?

Natasha reaches for Teddy's zip. Underneath, what should be mysterious to her, but is not. Those afternoons with Nico by the river, but they always stopped before—

Don't think. Just do it. Before it's too late.

'Are you on the pill?' says Teddy. 'It's just that I'm allergic to rubber, and, um, actually, can you stop doing that just for a minute because, in fact, oh dear, I'm going to—' He convulses, briefly, the last moments of a fish dying on a slippery deck.

'Oh.'

'Do you have any tissues?'

'No.' Natasha lights another cigarette. She thinks of Aunt Sonja. Is she involved in this? What if she never sees her again?

'Oh God,' says Teddy. 'What a mess.'

There's an old blue cleaning cloth stuffed in the corner of one of the windows. He takes that and starts dabbing at his lap. You'd think that—

There's a knock at the door. A sort of rattling. It's probably Tiffanie or one of the others come to see where Tash is, because they'd been planning to dance, and drink lots of prosecco and meet boys, other boys . . . It starts to rain, a soft pitter-patter on the roof of the summer house like the tiny hooves of something running away.

Natasha gets up and opens the door. And it's not Tiffanie, or one of the others.

It's Nico.

Tash almost doesn't recognise him at first, although his face is more familiar to her almost than her own. His hair has grown. He hasn't shaved. He looks rugged. Maybe in fact it isn't him? For a moment he blurs. But it is him. He smells clean.

'Who's this?' is the first thing he says, in Russian, looking at Teddy.

'This is Teddy Ross,' says Natasha, in English. 'His father is my father's lawyer. Um, Teddy, this is Nico, a friend from home.'

Natasha hopes Nico doesn't hold out his hand for Teddy to shake, not just because it would make him look stupid, but because Teddy's hands are still damp. He's also still holding the blue cloth. But it seems Nico has arrived from the sky like an angel, a real one, and real angels never look stupid even though they are holy and covered with feathers.

'What are you doing here?' she says to Nico, in Russian. He looks better than she remembered. It's not just the wings and the halo. He's taller, and tanned from the unexpectedly warm spring. His biceps blaze under his black t-shirt. Why exactly did she ever hate him? Without warning, her heart now fills with love. But it's too late. He's come for her, come all this way for her, flapping his heavy wings through the glair and the fluorescence, only to find her in the arms of a mortal man. Not even a man. A smug, coddled boy. And not even his arms: his hot fat sticky hands. Suddenly, Tash is breathing underwater, her lungs brimming with shame, soaking it all up and keeping it muffled and safe forever. The glory of it. The cold wet. Its teeth in her.

Her father. In prison. The money, gone.

Her boots are so cool but no one cares. She has no split ends. She wants to smoke a thousand cigarettes all at once, to die painfully and slowly. She should have said more prayers. Eaten more vegetables. Gone for walks in the countryside. She should have rolled down her school skirt and done her homework properly and

200

once she'd done all that she should probably have read those letters.

Nico takes in the scene in the summer house for a few more moments and then leaves.

'Fuck,' says Tash.

'Was that your Russian boyfriend?' asks Teddy, as she heads for the door.

Tash follows Nico past the marquee and into the house. He takes his jacket from where he has hung it on a hook by the door and, without looking behind him, opens the door and walks through it. He doesn't even slam it.

'Wait,' says Natasha, following him.

He doesn't look back. He walks in the light rain up the uneven country road, past Teddy's driver in the Merc, past a Cambridge taxi dropping off some of Danny's friends. There's a village pub by the river and he stops just beyond it, by the little hump-backed stone bridge. Water gurgles underneath like it's being squeezed out of a sponge. All the last drops.

When Tash reaches Nico, she sees he is crying. Why do all these men cry? Could he not be bleeding like the sultan, riding away sated but worn on his steaming horse? She wants something else for their end, but it is this.

'I'm sorry,' she says. She touches his arm, but he shakes her hand off.

'Don't,' he says.

'I—'

'I can leave tomorrow. It's not a problem. Just forget I was ever here.'

'Nico.'

'You never replied to my letters,' he says. 'And then the police came. I thought you needed my help . . . I wanted to come and see that you're all right.'

'Well, I'm not all right,' says Tash. 'My father's in prison, so.' She shrugs. 'Why didn't you just email me?'

'We said we wouldn't.'

'You said that. I didn't care. How did you even know where to find me?'

'I went to your school. I thought the authorities might be reading your emails because of your father. When I got there they told me it was the weekend you all go home, but then a lady said there was a party you might be at and one of your friends was still there and I spoke to her and she gave me the address. I mean, she has cancer or something? Rachel? So awful.'

'Wait. Rachel's still at the *school?* She's supposed to be here.'

The water gushes more loudly beneath them, the sound you get in your ears before you pass out. Nico puts his head in his hands and sort of freezes, like an emoji.

'Oh fuck. Shit. I've got to get back there,' says Tash.

She runs to the house and finds Tiffanie standing on her own by one of the ice buckets. She's trying to move to the music, but she's a surprisingly bad dancer. Will

Tash ever see Tiffanie again after it all comes out about her father? Perhaps not. But she loves Tiffanie too, she realises. All this love, all of a sudden.

'Rachel's still at school,' Tash says.

'No,' says Tiffanie. 'It's not possible. She must be coming here?'

'No.' Tash shakes her head. 'We've got to go back and, I don't know, do something. She's been on her own with him for ages now. Fuckfuckfuck.'

Teddy walks unsteadily in from the garden, the bottle of Cointreau in one hand, and his dinner jacket in the other. He's using the DJ to cover his wet trousers. The Cointreau is half gone.

'You're back,' he says to Tash. 'Hello again.'

'Look,' she says to him. 'We need your car and your driver. We have to go to our school, now. It's less than an hour away. It's really, really important.'

'Sure,' he says. 'Let's have a last-ditch road trip before the driver's sacked. Why the fuck not?'

Tash looks at Tiffanie and raises an eyebrow.

'Yes, I am come-*ange*.'

*

Nico sits in the front with the driver, who is also Russian. They drop him off in Cambridge. There must be an Airbnb there, right? Then a plane back to heaven. Tash, Teddy and Tiffanie are silent in the back of the Merc as it rides the weak plumes of fluorescence that streak down the motorway.

The school is half-lit, because of Exeat. Of the three hundred girls who usually inhabit the old buildings, maybe fifteen are left. Some of the final-year girls are revising in their study bedrooms. With A Levels so close they can't afford to go home. There is the odd Middle Eastern crushlet who can't get home and back in the time available. One of them is afraid of the ghost of Princess Augusta, whom she believes haunts her dorm at night, and so she has taken to sleeping on the spare mattress in Miss Annabel's room while the other girls are away. Miss Annabel has no idea why on earth she is being kind to this scrawny brown-grey girl who isn't even good at ballet, whose chin looks wrong, who already has fallen arches. But when someone is with her she is calmer too, and there are fewer bruises the next day.

And there is the girl who now sees the world in black and white because something has gone wrong with her eyes, and her legs are unsteady perhaps because she is an animal now, a thin wolf moving through the dry grass, past the sheep, which stink of shit and wool and earth, and which she would not eat even if she was a wolf, even if she was about to die. And he's waiting for her because it's time to do her final measurements and then after that the prize, because—

It's light, because it's nearly midsummer. But it's also soso dark. Raindark.

Later, in the distance, across the water, the sounds of cars crunching up the gravel driveway. But who would be coming at this time of night? The lake sparkling darkly with the car lights, and the promise of the treasure in its depths.

*

'You need to talk to someone,' says Dominic. 'Seriously.'

'I'm all right,' says Tash.

She's looking out at the lake for the last time. It's almost a week since it all happened. In a few minutes Aunt Sonja will be here, and then it will all be over. Dominic and Tony are leaving too. In fact, everyone is leaving. The school is being condemned again, possibly for good. The girls who want to will do their exams at the local comprehensive, which has been so very kind. And then after the summer break almost everyone will be enrolled at alternative independent schools and life will go on. Tiffanie's going to stay in Paris. She says she'll write, and maybe she will.

'You don't want to end up with it all suppressed, girlie.' Dominic approaches Tash, holding something out. 'My card,' he says. 'You know. In case.'

She doesn't take it. He waves the card in the air for a few moments and then puts it away in a little silver tin. Tash breathes in slowly. Why is he here? But of course everyone's been talking to her, these last two days. Mrs

Cuckoo, explaining that she always knew the headmaster was up to something, but didn't know who to tell. Miss White, saying that she should have recognised that Rachel had an eating disorder because, well, she struggled herself, back in her days at Cambridge. Even Miss Annabel, so ghost-like these days, took Tash's hand in hers and squeezed it and said *Thank you*. Not that Tash will ever see any of them again.

Tash had been the first one into the headmaster's house, and she'd seen everything, before he started smashing it up, and before Amaryllis Archer came and told everyone to leave and sealed everything off. The stark front room downstairs, with the charts laid out on the table, and the metal callipers on top of them. A shelf of copies of Dr Moone's self-published book *The Black Diamond*. All the way up the stairs, the walls hung with pictures of a painfully thin young woman in a white tutu. And then the bedroom walls with all the framed black and white photographs like an exhibition of victims of starvation or disease: young women with their ribs like something from a thrifty butcher's shop, their cheekbones looming like pale rockets out of their shrunken skulls, their coating of soft fur; all these women, different but the same, each one arranged, naked or partially clothed, on the bed with white sheets. A tripod set up by the bed, its cold hard steel. A large black camera. Rolls of film. The smell of the darkroom in the en-suite. The lake and the horse sculpture visible through the window. The occultation of everything in the house, and its bare shame, but the girl free now. The girl in the lake, swimming. The man inside, weeping.

'He never sold any of the pictures,' Amaryllis Archer had told Tash, when her interview at the police station was over and they were talking about what happened. 'Or shared them. Bianca Downlowe took pictures of some of the images herself – but of course you saw those on Instagram. Most men who take photographs like that, well, there's a more obvious reason for it.'

'I guess it was all to do with his wife?' said Tash. 'Most of the photos were of her.'

'Hmm,' said Amaryllis Archer. 'Yeah. I think you're right. She died in the lake too. I wonder if he encouraged her, or if he only started doing it afterwards, in a fucked up kind of remembrance.' She shrugged. 'Well, he's locked up now, so.'

'He must truly have thought there was something beautiful about the images,' said Tash. 'I don't understand it.' Except she did, because they *were* almost beautiful in their own way, if you didn't know what had happened to the women to get them like that, and what happened to them afterwards. And what it felt like. 'And he wrote a book about the black diamond. He must have believed in that too.'

'Do you think so? Really?'

'I don't know.' Tash looked at Amaryllis Archer, that evening wearing a maroon shirt with strange tassels coming off it, and a yellow neck-scarf. 'Why now?' Tash asked. 'Why Bianca, and then Rachel, both in the same year? I mean, if it was all about his wife who died so long ago.'

'Oh, there's been one or two every year since his wife drowned,' said Amaryllis Archer. 'But no one really notices schoolgirls with eating disorders. No one puts them together. No one reports what happens to them to the police. And anyway, most of the girls just got sent home or to clinics and never returned to the school. There was one poor girl who died, in 1986. She was going to be a ballerina, like Dr Moone's wife had been. And there was the one who was pulled from the lake in the 1990s. Jacqueline Driver, I think she was called.'

'And also Dr Morgan,' said Tash. 'I mean, he died.'

'Yes. And Dr Morgan,' said Amaryllis Archer.

Natasha stands by the lake now, under a clear blue sky. She is playing with her bracelet, opening and closing it around her wrist. The sunlight harks wontonly off the diamonds and shoots around the grounds of the school in little insignificant rays, millions and billions of them.

'You're not thinking of . . . ?' begins Dominic. 'I mean, you're not going to . . . ?'

'What, drown myself? What do you think? You're the expert.' Natasha sighs. 'I'm not rich any more. Do you think that's enough of a reason? My father's an oligarch, or was. He was probably involved in dark money. Anyway, now he's in jail in Russia and I might never see him again. I'm leaving school and, well, that's kind of sad. But I'm going to work for my aunt. It'll be fine. I've just got to decide what to do with this.' Tash takes the diamond bracelet off her wrist. Holds it up. It glints more urgently now, with more force. 'Do you want to know how much this cost? Not that much, actually. You'll be surprised. £65,000. Not enough to buy a house, even around here. But I bet you'd like it, wouldn't you? You'd accept it if I gave it to you.' She holds the bracelet out to Dominic, and he takes a step forward and reaches for it. She looks at it once more, at its shiny snakelike head, before she hurls it in the lake. Her throw's not bad; she's always had strong arms. 'You could swim for it,' she says, as she walks away. 'But you won't.'

ACKNOWLEDGEMENTS

This book came out of nowhere and surprised me and everyone around me. I want to thank all those who helped me while I was writing it. In particular I'd like to thank my partner Rod Edmond for his continuing love and support. My family have always been my biggest fans and I am so grateful for all their encouragement and love. Thanks to Mum, Couze, Sam, Hari, Nia, Ivy, Gordian and Ruth. I'm very grateful for all my wonderful friends, colleagues and students, particularly those who read and commented on my manuscript. Particular thanks are due to Amy Sackville, Simon Trewin, Sarah Parfitt, Katie Szyszko, Jennie Batchelor, David Flusfeder, Christina Clover, Charlotte Hanson, Nikki Bullock, Sue Swift and Alice Bates. Big thanks also to Teri Johns, who keeps me organised and sane.

I'd also like to thank my brilliant editor, Francis Bickmore, and everyone at Canongate, particularly Vicki Rutherford and Lucy Zhou, and Lorraine McCann for the wonderful copy-edit. Thank you also to my amazing agents, Cathryn Summerhayes and Luke Speed. I'm extremely excited to be working with Patrick Walters, Jamie Laurenson and Maria Nicholson at See-Saw Films to develop this book into a TV series. Thanks so much to all at See-Saw for having faith in my vision.

I am very lucky to have some brilliant supporters on Patreon. I'd like to thank all my patrons, but in particular, Sherlock Bones, Katie Visser, Gareth Watts, Kelly Shorter, Katharine Rivett, Evelina Pecciarini, Kathy McLusky, Jim Cappio, Andrew Leader, Amanda Beasley, Charlie Phillips, Devon Dunlap, Joe Butler, Marguerite Croft, Rob Ellis (who also provided a splendid proof-read for which I am very grateful) and, of course, Sarah Barnett and Glen.

patreon.com/scarthomas